# THE
# **DANCE**
## OF A
# **WINDMILL**

Benjamin Coxson

 FriesenPress

One Printers Way
Altona, MB R0G 0B0
Canada

www.friesenpress.com

**Copyright © 2022 by Benjamin Coxson**
First Edition — 2022

ISBN
978-1-03-916140-5 (Hardcover)
978-1-03-916139-9 (Paperback)
978-1-03-916141-2 (eBook)

*1. FICTION, LITERARY*

Distributed to the trade by The Ingram Book Company

# THE
# DANCE
## OF A
# WINDMILL

Wandering hiking boots
Digging into unseen trails
Mud grips its trespasser

Dusk falling like rain
Silent clouds hold grey mountains
One lone star shapes the sky

Trees doze in heaven
Dwelling in euphoria
Starlight wakes to peace

A sole leaf dances
Twirling, waltzing in moonlight
Trampled under footsteps

# Chapter 1

My shoes had too many holes, but the soles were still intact. They weren't comfortable, but they did the job—like many other things in my life. While driving, I fidgeted with my suitcase handle, flipping it back and forth nervously. Like my shoes, the suitcase was also well worn and secondhand; an emblem of a dove, stripped of its silver paint, sat underneath the handle.

The inside of the taxi was impeccably dark, especially in contrast with the sunny landscape outside. Outside of my window, grey dust and a dulled blue sign passed. It read, *Thanks for visiting, please come again soon.* As we left the town's border, the taxi driver hummed to the tune on the AM radio and drove along the winding highway. Farms, cottages, and lakes passed; however, the most striking feature of this land was the dark green forests that blanketed the rolling mountains. The road chased like a snake between two edges: the mountains on the left and lakes on the right. Railroad tracks and dilapidated telephone posts lay between them. Some posts were still standing while others were missing; often, a bald eagle sat upon a meticulously placed nest among the remains. As I looked toward an enormous emerald lake, I noticed the sun setting, causing a blinding reflection on the water. I was on my way to my aunt and uncle's farm in the southern interior of British Columbia.

"So, kiddo, do you have a name?" asked the elderly taxi driver in an abrasive, hoarse voice.

"Edward, sir," I responded no louder than necessary.

"Good to meet you, Edward . . . so you're staying with Matt and Emma?"

"Yes, sir."

"Hmm. How long are you staying?" He coughed a little.

"I don't know."

"Well . . . when does school start?"

"September 3, I'll be in grade twelve."

"Oh? So, you're going to be the graduating class of '96."

Those were all the words we exchanged during my ride. That was ok; I did not want to talk anyhow.

The taxi took a sharp left-hand turn off the highway toward a steep road traversing directly up the nearest mountain. Something small glittered in the distance and caught my eye. It looked like a tall metal tower with a spinning wheel on top. I had never noticed this structure before. This windmill reminded me of a wizard's spire in some fairy tale. We passed a couple of other properties, one of which stood out to me. A brass E&E was crafted as a sign indicating the entrance to a farm road. This sign stood out to me because its owners seemed like the only ones to make an effort to label their land. The rest of the roads only had a number—if they were lucky. Deep grooves cut into the dirt road, and moss crept up the nearby trees. I doubted the car's ability to get up the steep slope, but it managed with a few slips. Finally, the taxi stopped at a red metal gate.

"Go on, Edward; I've been paid. Say hello to Matt and Emma for me. I still owe them a couple of rides after last summer."

The driver quickly lifted my second suitcase and backpack out of the trunk, a surprise given his age. Saying no more, he took off back down the steep driveway. A rattling sound followed the taxi as it bounced down the incline and a purplish smoke spewed from its exhaust and hung like a ghost.

Towering trees surrounded either side of the road, casting dark shadows on the dirt; the red gate was part of a long wooden fence that carried on into the forest. This fence was also painted in the same bright crimson red. The mountain we drove up levelled out into a flat area before returning to a sudden incline well off into the distance. The farm was nestled in this flattened area like a fawn sheltered in tall grass. Lofty sunlight reached through the towering grey peaks of the mountain. This area was government land: untouched and undisturbed. This was a heavenly view to many people, but it was sad and abandoned to me.

The farmhouse was small, two stories, and was painted a faded whitish yellow. A wraparound porch draped the outside from all angles. Dust swirled the house, occasionally picking up the odd piece of paper or plastic and dropping it off later. This farm was like a permanent garage sale gone wrong: the side yard was littered with unusable appliances, tubs, sinks, and old trucks. Kittens played where an engine used to be in an old brown tractor. Pale smoke whispered out of the chimney and swirled off into oblivion.

Two roosters fought in a whirlwind of dust in front of me, completely ignoring my presence. I picked up my two suitcases and backpack and walked toward the gate. I tried to unlatch the gate from the post, but it had sagged with time. I grunted with frustration to push, pull, and lift it. Meanwhile, the aggressive birds moved behind my legs to the other side of the road. I groaned with annoyance as I struggled to raise my two suitcases and backpack over the gate. After climbing over, I turned back and gave the metal a hefty kick while gritting my teeth and clenching my hands into fists. Immutable anger rose into my chest, causing my eyes to squint and cheeks to flush.

A *CLANG* echoed through the forest and reverberated off the nearby mountain. The eyes of the roosters were on me; I had startled them out of their fighting frenzy. They eyed me sideways, as birds do, looking with one side of their head and then turning to look with another.

"What are you looking at?" I screamed at the birds. I mouthed a series of profanities just to make sure I was heard. I felt my chest tightening and my head pounding.

I kicked some rocks at them, and they fluttered away. I found a tire lug nut on the side of the road and threw it into the forest. Puffing myself up and brushing my hair backward, I picked up my suitcases and started to walk up the driveway in uneven ruts. There were sounds of animals but not of people.

I had never come here alone and was unsure where to go. After waiting a couple of minutes, I tightened my grip on the suitcase and took my first few steps up the porch. Much to my surprise, I was greeted by an enormous pig at the top. My anger drained as it became replaced with fear. I slowed my steps as I approached; each step creaked and groaned. The 400-pound monstrosity was lying on its side and breathing deeply. Its skin was caked with mud, and its tail twitched often. At first, I thought it was covered in blood, but I guess the red dirt from the farm had discoloured its skin—either that or it was sunburned. This was an unsettling picture. However, it did not move or wake up as I circled to get to the screen door. I quietly walked inside, not wanting to disturb the brute with a knock.

As I turned from the closed door, I saw a large belly bulging from a stained white shirt—a glimpse of my uncle before he picked me up and squeezed the breath out of me with a hug.

"It's great to see yah, Ed; I'm glad you're here. I'm sorry to hear what happened to your sister. Well, let's take your things and move them upstairs." He smelled like hamburgers and engine oil.

I flushed with anger at his words; how could he just bring up my sister and then leave it like that?

I struggled with my belongings up the stairs and went to the last door on the left. I accidentally tilted a couple of picture frames with my backpack; this was nearly unavoidable since the staircase was exceptionally tight. This was not my first time at my aunt and uncle's farm. When I was younger, we often came out here in the summer, but those days were gone. Mom and Dad would bring both of us to ride on ATVs and canoe on the lake. The summer days would get blistering hot, while the nights would cool off into a frost.

My new bedroom housed a sizable but broken grandfather clock, a dresser, a single bed, a mirror, and a small table. On top of the broken mechanical clock a digital one hummed, glowing at 8:27 p.m. in red. I set my suitcases on the bed and headed downstairs. As I awkwardly stood by the entrance, I noticed nothing had changed since I'd last visited the farm.

The clean and tiny kitchen housed a small fridge, oven, and table for two, although an additional chair was added with what little space was available. The kitchen was decorated in light yellow wallpaper and had a high ceiling. As for the living room, there was a chair, a rack with jackets, and a rifle. An old upright piano was stuffed into the corner, a TV with a hole through the screen sat next to the piano, and a Christmas cactus perched on a white window frame. Peering at this plant, I knew that it was neglected and had not bloomed. It just slouched in its pot. The house felt lonely and isolated but somehow peaceful at the same time.

"Here, eat this." My uncle pushed a couple of chocolate chip cookies into my hand. "Oh, and there is supper on the table."

I noticed a half-eaten chicken casserole in a dish on the counter. "When is Aunt Emma coming back?" I asked through a mouthful of cookies.

"Actually, I was about to call her; she should have been here by now."

The white screen door swung open with a crashing sound, and a collection of screeching followed it.

"I swear! Matt, I will shoot that pig of yours."

My aunt lay clutching her ankle in the front door. A set of broken teacups was sprawled across the floor like white rose petals. Peering out, I saw a pleased pig get up and move out of the middle of the porch. He seemed in no rush as he made his way down the steps into the fading night.

"Ed, help your aunt with those," my uncle said as he pointed to the floor and chewed a cookie.

I grabbed a broom and dustpan to clean the white shards off the floor. I tried to get them all, but some fell through the cracks, lodging themselves between hardwood flooring gaps.

The rest of the evening was filled with casual conversation and avoidance of why I was at my aunt and uncle's farm in the first place. I looked over an electric guitar magazine while my aunt filled in a crossword; my uncle just snored in his armchair. It was difficult to believe that my uncle and my mother were related—there was nothing similar between them outside their eyes and nose. Some of their sayings and speaking mannerisms were also uncanny. My uncle was always stouthearted and carefree, while my mother seemed nervous about everything. She would jump when my sister or I coughed or made a loud noise. She seemed to bear the world's weight on her shoulders, and unnecessarily so. She had this weird twitch when tired or stressed: jerking her hand upward. Finally, just before I declared that I was going to bed, my aunt piped up and stared at my uncle.

"I thought you had something you wanted to tell Edward," she said.

I looked down and shifted my gaze to my book while my uncle rubbed his eyes and turned uncomfortably in his chair.

"Uh, yeah. So, Ed, I wondered if you would be interested in working with me while you're here? We got a short summer this year, and I could use the help because we have some big projects to work on in the shop." He began to play with his reading glasses after an awkward pause.

"And? What else?" my aunt prodded.

"And, I wondered if you'd thinkin' it'd reasonable to talk to somebody. You know, a professional. Someone who knows how to deal with these things. We won't rush you—but just know what? There will be a time to get down to business."

I was going to have to tell a complete stranger about my problems. His imperfect speech came across loud and clear to me. They were probably going to analyze and diagnose me or lock me up. I would be professionally labelled as a problem . . . again.

*

Channels of anger, fear, and hopelessness gripped me without relent. Buried in heavy, scratchy wool sheets, I stared off into the stars through an open window while my aunt and uncle alternately snored. On the odd occasion, they snored in sync—a perfect harmony for someone who does not want to fall asleep.

Like everything else on the farm, brown dust and odd smells covered every inch of the space; I slept in an old bed that looked slightly more comfortable than the carpet below. The open window allowed a breeze to guide my curtains in a hypnotizing, slow-motion dance. Those ever-twinkling stars in the dark of the night seemed to offer hope in a pitiful place. I couldn't see this view back at the downtown apartments. The stars captivated me, pulling me away from my untameable thoughts. I fell asleep while eating granola bars and feeling the cold wind blow.

Crickets outside finished their harmony, and the peace of sleep fell on the farmland like a blanket. The peace of the land didn't transfer to my sleep. I had a nightmare. People came to a farm and killed some of the animals. Not this farm, but another one. I couldn't see what animals were there, or who did this. I just felt an uncontrollable rage and sadness. Then I realized it was a dream. Even still, I was very disturbed.

# Chapter 2

I woke up early not because I wanted to, but because the birds were bellowing outside my window. Each type of bird seemed to compete to be the most obnoxious and loudest of its neighbours. My mind was racing, but my body was weighed down. Rubbing my face, I groaned. I knew I could not get back to sleep. Sometimes I woke clutching my heart as it pounded away. I was infuriated that my body couldn't relax. There was no reason for panic. I was not a crazy person.

I listened for my aunt and uncle, but I didn't hear anything except outside animals and wind rustling through the leaves. I opened the window a bit more and leaned out to see if anyone was around . . . No one. I hopped out of the window and scurried out onto the roof. I slowly made my way to the side opposing the road, careful not to make too much noise.

The sun was beginning to peek out from the distant horizon, causing the town and nearby windmill to shimmer. This was the same windmill I saw from the mountain's base the day before. I sat in jeans and a t-shirt for about an hour, the damp cold biting at my bones but the warming sun lighting up the back of my neck. While looking at the town, I drew out some cigarettes and a lighter. Already my hands were stiff, and it was difficult to get a flame. I felt a little calmer, but my mind was still racing. My thoughts were rushing like a thousand minnows in a stream—clearly present but unable to be grasped. The only thing left to do was panic and calm down, then rinse and repeat.

"What am I doing?" I asked myself as I looked down at the ground below.

I wasn't worried about the height; I needed a bit of an escape from the house. It felt so neutral.

*KNOCK KNOCK!*

Can't people just leave me alone? I could hear a loud and heavy knocking on my door through the open bedroom window. This was my uncle's way of startling my sister and me when we visited the farm when we were little.

"Breakfast is ready when you are, Ed," Uncle Matt bellowed through the door.

I panicked to inhale the remains of my second cigarette and put it out on the eaves trough before swinging back into my room.

Although it was still reasonably cold, I wore a fleece over

my t-shirt, shorts, and sandals. I wasn't used to wearing footwear in the house, but it was expected on the farm. Looking in the mirror, I quickly sprayed on a manly blue cologne to mask the smell of cigarettes. I knew I wasn't supposed to be smoking at my aunt and uncle's house, but they hadn't said anything the night before. Besides, I needed to calm down; technically, I wasn't indoors. As I brushed back my long, black hair, I noticed cracks in the bottom of the mirror. Near these cracks, a black and white photograph was inserted into the frame: a picture of a river. This river didn't seem beautiful or unique. In fact, the photo was horrendous, yet someone had decided to value it.

I made my way downstairs and noticed an upside-down five-gallon pail next to the table. A boy sat on top of it with his back turned to me. I didn't think that everyone was up. Had they seen me sitting on top of the roof? Had they seen me smoking? Which direction had the boy come from? I knew there was a path from the back of the farm; however, I didn't know if he had come from that direction. I hadn't seen him approach through the woods, but I hadn't been expecting to see anyone wander onto the property from anywhere besides the main road.

Aunt Emma turned and beckoned me to the table. "Please sit down, Edward; this here is our neighbour, Adam."

The boy swung around on his bucket and looked at me. He had dirty blond hair and a round face and was very slender. His glasses were crooked and smudged, and he wrinkled his nose as he looked at me. He wore a white shirt with horizontal blue stripes, blue jeans, and dusty black cowboy boots. He was a little younger than me but taller. Adam seemed like the type of person who would have been a geek if he had grown up in the city. I didn't know what they called those types of people here.

"How do you do?" he asked me as he stood out and extended a hand after wiping it on his jeans. I shook his hand and looked at my aunt. I didn't say it, but I hadn't expected to see people so soon. I just wanted to be alone and get back home. Somehow I knew that my aunt understood this, as she looked at me with a sympathetic expression.

"Ah, I'm pretty good; how about you?" I answered in a deeper voice and flat tone.

"Well, I'm doing pretty good, we got a new horse last night and I got to ride her here." Adam tossed his thumb over his shoulder, pointing behind his back. I looked through the screen door, but I couldn't see anything. However, the sunburnt pig made direct eye contact with me through the screen and gave a snort. It gave a small stomp with its front legs and raised its chin to look at me with its beady black eyes. I stopped midchew through a piece of bacon.

"Adam's here for breakfast, I thought he could show you around the town and where he lives. Maybe introduce you to some people?" my aunt piped up.

"Sounds all right with me," I responded with indifference.

As we ate breakfast, I asked where my uncle was. Aunt

Emma explained that he was doing extra work at his shop. My aunt and uncle owned a metalworking shop in the nearby town. This town had roughly 1500 people and was called Cherry Lake. While my uncle spent most of his days at the shop, my aunt worked the farm and took care of some of the accounting aspects of the business.

Breakfast was bacon, eggs, and fruit, all from the farm. I had always thought it was interesting when people had a connection with making their own food. Although it's hard to describe, something about plastic and modern food preparation seemed disgusting. All those neat little slices of bacon put side by side at the supermarkets or the rows of perfect cans.

"Thanks, Emma," Adam announced as he finished his plate, picked it up, and made his way over to the kitchen counter. He then immediately began washing his plate, fork, and spoon. After he finished, he took my plate and started cleaning it too, without me asking.

Adam and I stepped outside, and he whistled. The air was a bit warmer now, about an hour since I'd crawled out of my bedroom window. I looked in anticipation of Adam's whistle: what was he whistling to? Nothing happened . . . He just softly looked off into the distance, and then his absent-minded gaze fell to his left-hand side.

"Oh yeah," he muttered and straightened his hat. "New horse . . . Help me look for it, won't you?"

"What are we looking for?"

"Four legs, long neck, and a tail. Whitish. The name's Shadow."

"I know what a horse is."

"I thought Emma said yous were from the city?"

"We aren't dumb there; we know what animals are."

"I'm just teasing; calm down, cowboy." Adam poked me in the back with a teasing gesture.

"Sheesh," I muttered, loud enough to make sure that Adam heard me.

Once we found the horse, Adam offered me a ride, but I declined. I said that I fell off a horse last time. This wasn't true; I didn't know how to ride and didn't want to make a fool out of myself. Besides, my sister had fallen off a horse and broken her arm a couple of years ago.

As we neared the mountain slope, we passed chicken coops, the pigpen, and a barn. The uncountable rows of trees were intimidating. Patches of blue lupine flowers dotted the area. The last man-made structure in this direction was the windmill, which creaked and groaned with every move. This structure seemed to bother me, but I couldn't tell why. Adam didn't notice. A lone rabbit under the windmill watched us as we passed.

I walked while Adam rode his horse and indicated that we were going to his farm. Adam's family were neighbours to my aunt and uncle; their farm was to the west. There was a dirt trail from one farm to the next, and it took about forty minutes to walk there. I didn't mind because it felt peaceful.

We travelled in the shadow of the mountain, the sun still in the east. This made the summer air quite cool but tolerable once I began to get my heart rate up. A long stripe of red mud lay down the middle of the path, sometimes growing wider and sometimes disappearing altogether, though the red line remained constant throughout our journey.

Shadow was a short white horse who swayed while he walked. Although he was older, there seemed to be energy in his eyes. His tail would flick as we talked, and he appeared patient and kind.

"So why did you name the horse Shadow?" I mentioned it after a while. "Isn't it the wrong colour?"

"Actually, he is the perfectly correct colour," Adam responded. "And technically, he is more of a shade than colour."

"How do you mean?" I asked.

"Well, when we were going to pick him up, we were looking at a couple different horses. My dad was super interested in this Missouri Fox Trotter, but he wanted to see all the options. The guy selling them said there was one more, but he couldn't see where it was. He only knew it was a white one. It turns out that the horse was standing right by a building painted white. The only way we could see him was because of his shadow. The sun was strong that day. So here he is, the white horse: Shadow." Adam gave a full smile, leaned forward, and patted Shadow's neck. "Licorice?" Adam pulled a package from his bag and offered me a string.

"Nice," I said. I shook my head at the licorice offer.

I didn't have anything to add to the story or conversation. Adam was like an alien to me. I didn't know anything about horses, breeds, or even farms. For the remainder of the walk, we talked about school, where we grew up, and the sports we were interested in. Oddly enough, Adam was very involved in wrestling, even though he didn't seem to have the body for it. He appeared to be composed of more skin and bones than muscle. Once we started talking about wrestling, there was no stopping his monologue until we reached his home. I didn't mind because he didn't ask why I was staying with my aunt and uncle; somehow he steered the conversation around that awkward detail as if he knew what to talk about. I wondered if Aunt Emma told him something. This led to an irrational flare of anger that quickly disappeared.

"Aaaaaaaah!!" I cried with surprise as I slid down the path. I had misjudged my step and lost traction down a steep hill. I continued to slide on my back, down the middle of the trail. Trees blurred in the corners of my vision, and all I could see was the bottom. As I eventually came to the end of the slope, I heard Adam laughing and snorting.

"I see you found our natural slip 'n' slide—I guess I should have warned you to get some real shoes on before we left."

"Arrr," I growled and got up. Turning to my back, I saw mud was lathered completely down my shirt and pants. Cuts on my hands began to ooze. I shook the dirt off my fingertips and wiped the rest off with nearby moss.

Adam regained his voice. "Don't worry, I'll let you borrow some of my clothes when we get to my place. Come on now." This time he passed me a licorice strand from the bag. It was super old; I could snap it in half with my hands.

I didn't tell Adam this, but I had severe doubts about his fashion sense and wondered if I would come out looking like a clown. There was no way other people could see me here. I couldn't make a bad impression on my first day. Plus, that would be social suicide once I started school.

It was not long until we reached his farm. I wanted to smoke, but I said and did nothing; at home I would have just lit one up. I was surprised at what I could see. The end of the path opened to a large expanse, and trees peeled away. There was a vast, tidy orchard with neat rows of trees sorted by type. The ground beneath them was clean and perfect. I had expected Adam's farm to have the same dilapidated appearance as my aunt and uncle's. In addition to the orchard, a long, white fence was drawn from the forest up to the farmhouse. Within the pasture, sheep were grazing. This pasture was massive and flourished with rich, green grass. Perhaps the only repulsive aspect of the farm was the smell of the sheep; however, that was hardly noticeable compared to the cleanliness of the rest of the area. Rows of grapes grew between the orchard and farmhouse. It was also on the mountainside like my aunt and uncle's farm, but the land was not as flat. The entire area was situated downward while the farmhouse stood on the top. It matched the neatness and perfection of the farm. Compared to my aunt and uncle's, it was a large house, with a sizable porch attached to the upper floor. There were two levels: a walkout basement and a second floor with large windows.

A figure moved about on the porch in odd positions. The person looked at an enormous object on the deck and seemed to be carrying it around.

"Oh hey—that's my dad; I'll introduce yah," Adam said after concluding his wrestling monologue.

Adam rode his horse to the house, where he hitched it to a post near the basement doors. This was where we entered. It shocked me to see Adam just walk in. No one seemed to know about the invention of keys in this small, rural area. Did they really feel that safe? While the inside was older-looking, it was impeccably clean. Three brown leather couches were arranged in a crescent shape in the room with a large TV mounted on the wall. Five deer heads were mounted on the opposing one. A pool table was placed behind the couches, and behind there were bookshelves absolutely packed with books and board games of every kind imaginable. Perhaps this was the only messy part of the room. The sheep were dirty outside, and the books were disorganized inside. I supposed that was how things ought to be.

Taking the stairs two at a time, Adam sprang up to the main level.

"Hey, Dad, I brought Edward back with me," Adam bellowed.

As I chased Adam up the staircase, I turned the corner to see Adam's father stepping inside and looking in Adam's direction. Suddenly I felt nervous, although I didn't know why. Adam's father was barefooted, wearing blue jeans and a black shirt with a band label that I had never heard of. One of the most prominent, striking features were his large, clear, grey eyes. They were somewhat unnerving. He just smiled and nodded upward. I felt that I could hold no secrets from him. It was a gut reaction, and I felt uneasy.

I thought back to my own dad, and it was as if I were sucked out of my body and mind for a couple of seconds before becoming aware of the situation.

# Chapter 3

"Wanna see something cool?" Adam's dad asked.

"Uhhh . . . sure?" I responded while thinking of my entire backside caked in mud.

"Here, both of you, come outside with me." Adam's father beckoned enthusiastically.

The three of us stepped out onto the porch. The property's beauty was my first shock; the second observation was the size of the deck. It was absolutely massive. I was surprised because it was almost the exact size as the entire downstairs. The farm was beautiful from below, but the farm looked even grander from up here.

"Here, take a look at this."

I looked around; projects lined the entire outside of the deck. Adam's dad was beckoning to a large, cylindrical object in the corner. Although the thing in the corner looked interesting, I couldn't pry my eyes away from the other objects lining the deck. There was a bubbling green vat, a tangle of wires, and a mechanical hand on the patio table. A grey parrot sat upon the deck's handrail and was muttering something to itself. Lastly, a spinning blue object was floating above a solid metal cube, suspended in . . . nothing?

"I just adjusted it today, we should be able to see some stuff." Adam's father pointed to several knobs.

"See some stuff?" I asked.

"Oh yeah, I guess I should tell you what it is. You see, this is a telescope I bought secondhand from the university. One of my friends is a professor there; sometimes they must sell their old equipment. He called me last week saying they are getting some new telescopes and need the rest of the old ones gone. So I drove up there with my pickup and got it for an amazing deal. There's only one catch. For three nights over the next couple of months, I will need to host a student or two because the university is researching and wants some extra eyes on their investigation. I have no idea what they are doing."

"That sounds really neat," I responded with my arms crossed and brow furrowed.

Adam's father seemed to take offence and smirked. "Seriously—out of all the words you could use to describe this thing, you use the word *neat*? This is an instrument of the heavens; we can see the indescribable and unknowable. I'm sure that whatever we see through here would dwarf any art human hands could make. And the coolest thing: we get to take photos through it!"

He held up a small, steel tube.

There was an unusual pause, but it didn't phase him.

"Sir . . . so . . . that's . . . the camera?" I ask while trying to convince myself not to feel stupid.

Laughing, Adam's dad responded, "Edward, firstly, call me Ethan, and secondly, this is a metal tube." He gave a slight chuckle.

Adam chimed in, "Yeah, that tube actually fits onto my new camera and then goes onto the telescope's eyepiece. At least, that's what we are told. Do you want to come by tonight and see how it works?"

Typically, this type of thing would not interest me. Actually, this thing still did not interest me, but I figured it was better than sitting around doing nothing. These people seemed different from those I was used to being around. Maybe another type of manliness.

"Adam, why don't you get Edward a new outfit, and I can drive you into town. You could show him the school. I need to pick up some flowers and things anyway."

My suspicions were correct; I walked out of Adam's house and climbed into the truck's front seat wearing wet runners, too-long jeans, and a shirt that should not have been approved for mass production. The shirt was baggy with blue and purple, separated by a diagonal line. Adam was in the backseat, and his father looked through several CDs. An elderly Labrador retriever sat beside Adam.

We drove from the farm and down the same steep mountainside that I had arrived on the previous day. The pickup truck was fancy, well, at least as fancy as farm trucks could be. Did Adam's family have lots of money? I felt like I was in a completely different mindset; for a while, the worries of the present and future slipped away, and I found myself excited to see Cherry Lake.

I didn't remember much from my past visits, but I did remember a couple of places in the town. When my sister and I got bored at the farm, we begged Mom to take us there. There wasn't much to do, but we always did the same thing: thrift store shopping, walking by the lake, and visiting Uncle Matt's steelworking shop. Sometimes they would be working on machinery, other times they would be working on things for the railroad or even automotive jobs. Uncle Matt once made a bike for me a couple of years ago—it wasn't painted, and it was stuck in the same gear, but I remember being so impressed with it. I felt proud that someone in my family made something so special. It all seemed silly when I looked back on it.

The town was established in 1929 due to the mining, farming, and lumber trade that began after the war. There weren't too many streets in Cherry Lake; most of the town was shaped like a horseshoe, cupping the lake from which it got its name. The railroad tracks that hugged the highway also ran straight through the town, mainly in the industrial area. That was just about all I could remember—I learned nearly everything about Cherry Lake from the small, volunteer-run museum. A museum was a generous title; it was more like a taxidermy showcase. Although I hated school, there was something extraordinary about the museum. Maybe I could go back sometime? It wouldn't be as fun as before; too much had changed.

"All right, here it is," Adam's dad spoke up as he pulled into the school's parking lot. A train passed behind it, and telephone poles lined either side of the street leading up to the parking lot. It hardly appeared inviting, and it was worse off than the school at home.

Adam and I jumped out of the truck and just stood taking in the rest of the school. Although it now appeared to be in a neglected state, I could see that it was once a grandiose building. The front of the building hosted several pine trees and was covered with sandstone. Two tall wooden doors framed the entrance.

"Well, wanna check it out?"

"Don't we need someone to be here?" I gestured to the empty parking lot and noticed that Adam's dad was now out of sight down the road.

"Ha, no one locks anything around here." Adam strutted up the front steps and opened the doors. "It makes crime less fun."

"Apparently," I said, shocked. "You would lock up your bike, both tires, and take the bike seat with you where I lived. Maybe even take a pedal off if that was an option."

We entered through the main entrance: wooden doors discoloured from the intense summer sun paired with their transparent wood stain. A black rug and metal-slatted flooring covered the lobby. The ceiling was also relatively high. In the main hallway, dented faded-yellow lockers lined both sides, occasionally interrupted by a wooden door frame: the entrance to a classroom. I noticed from outside that there were two rows of windows and guessed there was an upstairs. Perhaps the most notable thing about the inside of the school was the floor. It was a sizeable, speckled tan and dull red tile that made people look like chess pieces. It had warped over time, creating small ripples or waves in the near-perfect shine of the waxed floors.

"Come on, I'll show you around." Adam strutted enthusiastically. "Ok, first is the office; you probably will need to go here to sign up for classes during the beginning of school. We already got our schedule figured out back in June. Here's the music room, and across from it is the library—terrible positioning, if you ask me. Down here is the science lab, and there are a couple of classrooms. These are the stairs to the second level; nothing here is interesting, only social studies and math classrooms." His cowboy boots made blunted, marching noises on the floor as he walked. "And here is the downstairs; I gotta show you this."

He took each step down quickly; I was amazed that he could shuffle down the stairs in those boots. At the bottom, he took a sharp left and pointed to something.

"Please admire this spectacle of strength," he said in a goofy tone.

He was pointing to a dimly lit display case. Down at the bottom sat a couple of crests and a trophy which said *1995 Wrestling Provincial Champions: Cherry Lake Public School.* The award was golden and had an angel on top lifting an orb with both hands.

"See that one there, on the far side?"

"*Adam M.*, whoa, I guess you really are good—I mean, you really seem into wrestling." I was genuinely impressed.

"Yeah, I had to fight a gargoyle of a man to get any points for my team."

We continued the tour downstairs. Adam showed me the wrestling room and the workshop. Metalwork was positioned on one side of the enormous room, while woodworking was set on the other half. Down on the very far side of the dimly lit hallway, the stairs moved upward to one last entrance. This was a lane pool—quite surprising because it seemed out of place. It was enormous, and a swim schedule was posted near the entrance. I noticed some dark spots that needed cleaning, and the pool had a greenish tinge to its blue. Above the pool was a glass room much like a greenhouse, which arched over the top of the pool. Ripples of sunlight bounced off the ceiling, refracting through the glass. The glass needed some cleaning as well. The semicircle opening on the other side of the pool led to an exit.

An old man wearing florescent green swim shorts laboured

through a backstroke back and forth in the lane pool. He moved at a snail's pace but remained afloat. He didn't seem to notice us when we walked in or when Adam talked.

"Here it is, the pride of Cherry Lake High: the pool. Except we can only afford to keep it open half the year, it lets too much heat out during the winter." Adam gestured to the roof. I kicked the water with my shoe while pointing and sneering at the old man who didn't realize we had entered.

After exiting the building, I asked, "Do you mind if I take a smoke?" There was a soccer field outside the pool exit, and past this, a field of brown cows.

"You smoke? Whoa," Adam responded with more curiosity than judgment. "That's not a good idea, they are really strict about that sort of thing on the school campus—you better not." I lit one up anyway, looking at Adam and then glancing away. So what if I got caught? What were they going to do? Suspend me? No one cares.

We walked back down the road to the school and then toward the lake. We passed a garage and a furniture store, crossing old and unused railroad tracks. I put my cigarette out there. Once we passed a couple of houses, we finally stood, leaning on the dock overlooking the lake. The dull *thunk* of wooden wind chimes tumbled in the breeze; these were positioned on the wharf below a gas lantern. Fishing gear clattered in the wind along with seagulls evaluating their luck at stealing from the boats.

"Why do you smoke?" Adam asked.

"Why don't you?" I replied.

"Fair enough," Adam responded and scratched behind his ear.

I didn't know what to say; it was an awkward pause between us. I knew it, and he did too. I flicked some paint chips from the dock into the water.

*Honk!* Adam's dad was driving by. "Hey, boys, jump in!" he said while beckoning us to come over.

We hopped into his pickup truck and started down the road, now with me in the backseat and Adam in the front. The golden Lab just smiled through panting and let me pet him.

"Nice flowers you got this time." Adam pointed to a bouquet in the center console.

"Thanks, they had a bit more of a selection today." Adam's father smiled.

We started to head back toward the high school, but instead of continuing straight, we took a left and came to a large, nearly windowless building. It looked rather plain: two stories of a greyish brown with yellow accents. The roof was slanted upward toward the freshly paved parking lot. An ancient oak towered behind the facility, floating in the breeze.

"You can come in, Edward, if you want," Adam's father mentioned over his shoulder.

"What are we seeing?"

"It's 'Who we are seeing,' and the 'who' is little Leah, my youngest," Adam's father responded and nodded.

"Yeah, sure, I can come." I hadn't caught the sign outside and was curious about this building. The front doors opened, and a man in a wheelchair was pushed out by a nurse. We all got out of the truck, and I began to tremble in my hands and tear up.

Is this a hospital? I can't go in there! I thought to myself. "Coward," I muttered under my breath. I felt for the pack of cigarettes in my pocket, turning them around in my fingers. With the other hand, I began to make a snapping motion with my fingers, but without noise. My whole body shook, and my mind brought up pictures and images from the past. Adam and his father started walking toward the entrance. The purple and red flowers drooped in the breeze. I turned around and ran my fingers through my hair—I just need to grow up, be a man, and get this over with. Faking my confidence, I gathered my frustration and fears and caught up with the others.

# Chapter 4

The interior confirmed my worst suspicions; it was indeed a hospital. When I walked through the doors, I noticed Adam's dad talking to a lady behind the counter while Adam looked at a poster. Both seemed unnaturally calm and collected.

Flashbacks of past hospital experiences filled my mind, and I spaced out in a daze while standing in the entranceway. I remember when my sister fell off the horse and broke her arm. We went to the hospital around lunchtime. It was night by the time we left. There probably were about thirty-five people in that emergency room. Every chair was filled, and people leaned against the walls or squatted on the ground. Nurses hustled to and fro like sailors trying to bail out a ship destined to sink. This was the natural and expected state of healthcare back home. Busy, not slow. Alarming, not quiet.

"Get out of my way, boy, I'm coming through," said a raspy voice behind me. An old man stumbled toward the entrance with a security guard running after him. The old man was dressed in a brown suit, black tie, dress shoes, and an umbrella. While he ran, his umbrella fumbled in unusually shaky hands. He muttered under his breath, "It's pouring outside, and I'm late—she's going to be so mad at me."

"Who . . . wait, it's not raining," I stammer, confused by his attire and what the man had said. The old man's shuffle was slow and laboured. He didn't seem to care; he was out of the door before I could do or say anything. The security guard chased him and caught him in the parking lot.

Adam's dad turned around and noted my distressed and confused look. "Oh, don't worry about him, he's just mistaken. We see him almost every time."

"Does he always carry an umbrella?" I asked.

"Actually, whenever I come here, he does; it seems like he is waiting for something, or something is waiting for him."

The lady behind the desk piped up. "And we don't actually know why he is in a rush. He always has somewhere to go but never talks about it. And he has been here for quite a while." She just gave a chuckle and shook her head.

We made our way down the hall, following a light blue line. The inside of the clinic was impeccable. The floors were clean, the walls were perfect, and everything was orderly. Perhaps too orderly. After my fright with the old man, my thoughts started to sink back into where I was. My heart was pounding. I had to command my thoughts: Get a grip. Get a hold of yourself.

We finally reached the next desk.

"Ahh, Ethan and Adam, welcome back. Who do you have here?" The speaker was a very short and very young nurse. Someone who looked far too young to be in the position; however, she had a squeaky voice of authority and confidence.

"This is Edward; Edward, this is Becky."

"Nice to meet you, Edward," Becky responded. "You two know where to go; I'll sign you in." It seemed that Adam and his father were regular attendees of the clinic.

We stopped at room 213 and went in. I don't know what I was expecting, but I certainly was not expecting this. A small ten-year-old girl held a knitting magazine, wore a baseball hat, and sucked on a lollypop. She wore loose, baggy clothing and had her feet propped up on a stool. A rhythmic metallic device by her side was making a slow whirling noise. This big device extended opaque, white tubes connected to her arm. From the positioning of the baseball cap, I could tell she had no hair. Her skin was blotchy and yellow, and her eyes seemed grey and dulled. I felt sick looking at her despite her appearing clearly comfortable. In the room, there was a bed and a tiny side table. Notes, cards, books, and a stack of VHS tapes were scattered around the room's corners. This mess resembled a bedroom rather than a perfectly cleaned hospital.

A crystal vase on the table was filled with one dozen

wilted pink roses. Adam's dad took the pink roses and tossed them into the garbage.

"Hey, kiddo—look what I got you now!"

The little girl beamed from ear to ear and looked between Adam, his father, and me.

"Hey, I'm Leah," she introduced herself as she looked curiously at me. She seemed a little shy.

"Hi," I responded, took an absent-minded pause, and looked around the room. "I'm Edward."

"Hey, Adam—did you see that Bill is here?"

"Bill? When did you see him?" Adam looked around frantically. "Hang on, I gotta talk with him."

"That way." Leah pointed to the left of the room's entrance.

"Edward, do you mind keeping Leah company?" Adam's dad asked. "I just need to get these flowers some water."

"I'm fine here," I lied.

"Great, I'll be back in a couple minutes."

As soon as Adam's father left, I stood in the doorway, looking down at my fingers and wringing my hands. I didn't know what to do or say. I thought I was terrified before—now it was worse.

"So, I've never seen you before," said Leah. She seemed to get over any type of shyness.

"Nah, I just got here yesterday; I'm living at my aunt and uncle's farm. Their names are Matt and Emma."

Leah put down her magazine and suddenly appeared excited. "The neighbours? I didn't know that they had family. I just . . . thought that they just . . . kind of did their own thing."

"My family hasn't come back to the farm lately."

"Why did you stop?"

"Because . . . we couldn't make it. What is that thing?" I asked to redirect the topic.

"This is Bartholomew, the blood dialysis genie. He takes my bad blood, sorts it out and shoots me full of the good stuff." Leah slapped the top of the machine and smiled at it. "We met two years ago, and the relationship has been growing ever since."

Bartholomew had rounded triangles that turned and passed like clockwork. As I stepped closer, I could see more tubes and medical equipment. Now I felt physically sick and looked around the room, trying not to look at Leah. I felt terrible that I could not look at her, but I didn't have much choice. I ended up looking out of the window and fidgeting with my hands.

"Why don't you sit down?" Leah asked with a forced smile. I was probably pale.

"Yeah, thanks," I responded as I took an oversized visitor's chair. I wished Adam and his dad were back by now. "So . . . how did you get the name Bartholomew?" The lump in my throat started to shrink, but my heart pounded.

"Well, you see, I guessed that he looked like a Bartholomew and the name started to catch on. Some of the nurses started to use the name, especially since this is the only machine for the hospital. I gave him googly eyes, but someone took them off."

She smiled, and I looked back to the window.

"I wasn't always here. I got sick two years ago." She held a long pause. "I think I'm losing this fight. I'm losing to Mr. Wilms. It's ironic when you look up the meaning of my name."

"Mr. Wilms? What type of sickness is that?"

"Technically, nephroblastoma. Plus a little extra something else on the side."

"A who?" I questioned.

"Exactly—who knows?"

I looked at her confused, and she smiled and looked at some cards that hung on a string against the wall.

Leah stared intensely at these cards. "I'm not sure exactly what's happening. The doctor has a name for my sickness, but that doesn't really help my situation, right? I actually think that it is worse for my family. I've been sick for so long, and I just wish it was over or I could move on with it. I know I will die. I hope no time soon . . . but I guess I've had a long life if it's my time."

I was disgusted, confused, shocked, and frustrated at the same time.

"That was a joke." She smiled with her eyes.

"Huh?" I responded.

"Long life. I'm ten. Hey, wanna hear another joke?"

I sat there for a couple more minutes listening to Leah's

jokes and riddles. I didn't know what to do, so I just sat there and paid attention. At one point, Leah started to violently cough with whole-body convulsions. The tubes hooked up to her bounced in response to her movements. My sick feeling returned, and I froze in my seat unable to do anything. I still wanted to run, but that was for my own sake. For me to stay, that was for Leah. Adam's father reappeared shortly after the third joke, holding a new vase and trimmed flowers. He smiled with kindness and pride that I'd never seen or expected from him.

As we drove back to Adam's farm, I sat in the back seat and repeatedly flipped a coin in my hand. I squished a hamburger wrapper into the cupholder. It started raining gently, and I pressed my head against the window to look down the road. I'd left the hospital—I got away, but I still didn't know what I wanted. I had wanted to go so badly, and now I got it. I was angry at the existence of life itself. How can someone so young experience so much pain? Life can be cruel; I didn't need to be reminded about that.

"Here, I got something for you," Adam's father said as we pulled up to the house. He ran to the shed attached to the house, rummaged inside, and pulled out a compound bow.

"This is for you. Everyone in the family has one, and I figured things may get dull while you visit here. Life can sometimes be slow at Cherry Lake, so I thought it would be a great idea to learn something new."

"I . . . I don't know what to say. Thank you!"

"Well, technically, it was Leah's, but now it's yours. We bought it secondhand, but I tested everything, and it seems like it's in great condition."

That afternoon Adam taught me how to use the bow, and afterward, I stayed for supper. Although I was grateful for the gift, I felt awkward and discomforted at Adam's father's present. Leah was just in the hospital, why wouldn't he hold onto it for when she gets out? We had some fruit from the orchard and some sausage. When the sun started to set, we tried to focus the new telescope on the rising moon but had difficulty getting it to work. Finally, I declared my journey home. I asked to go alone. Adam's father refused and insisted that Adam could walk me halfway. "There are things with big teeth in the forest, don't you know?" He made fangs with his fingers and had a half-serious, half-joking look. I looked at Adam across the deck, and he just continued to poke at the ground with a stick. He gave a faint smile, which somewhat unnerved me.

# Chapter 5

In the dusk, Adam marched me back home, this time without a horse but with a gun. The setting sun's orange glow contrasted with the rising moon's fluorescent illumination. Both light sources drew soft shadows of duelling shades: warm and cold colours. I felt uneasy, both with the gun and what hid in the forest. *Big teeth*. Those words stuck in my mind, ideas of creatures slinking in the shadows.

"Adam, what's in these woods?" I asked nervously as leaves crunched under our feet.

"Oh, nothing that you need to be worried about. Still. It doesn't hurt to be a little extra cautious." He patted his rifle on the stock. I still looked at him as we marched on, unsatisfied with his answer. Looking at my wide eyes, he refined his response. "We got coyotes, bears, wolverines, lynx, and cougars."

"Bears?" I questioned with a quavering voice.

"Oh, those aren't too bad. You see, most times they are actually quite nice—if you leave them alone and give them a little respect, they will treat you fine. I'm worried about cougars. I've only seen one once, but I bet they have seen me loads of times. They are so quiet that you don't really stand a chance. There are so many deer around here that I wouldn't worry much about them. Like I said, it doesn't hurt to be a little extra cautious."

As we walked in the setting twilight, Adam stayed the entire way. I didn't ask him to, but I think he knew I was not used to the woods. I felt a tremble in my step, not visible, thankfully, because that would be pathetic.

"All right, I guess I'll see you around?" Adam asked.

"Yeah, tell your dad thanks." I held up the bow and three arrows in my right hand.

"Of course!" Adam turned back to the trail, walking by himself in the direction of the setting sun. His shadow was long, and the sun painted the area in orange pastels.

I stopped at the barn and saw the giant pig sleeping, sprawled across the ground on straw. Some light was visible through the cracks of the barn rafters.

"I could go anywhere, you know," I said as I looked at the pig. "I could leave everything behind me and go to New Brunswick or north to Yellowknife. I look old enough to pass as eighteen. I could get a job somewhere where no one knows me or just drift from city to city. I could live out on the snowy plains and see miles around me. I would watch the dancing lights in the sky. Nothing but the cold, harsh air and eternal sky. I could make it . . . I don't need no one." The pig's only response was the flick of a tail and a groan.

I stopped behind the farm's workshop and lit up a cigarette. Despite the short walk from the barn to the house, I was petrified. Halfway, a sound in the dark made my heart jump into my throat. Each creak and flutter set my heart ablaze.

*Hsssssfght.*

The sound came from inside the workshop. I looked around the corner to see a flickering blue light dance across the entrance. Some streams of fog flowed into the farmyard like a giant apparition falling asleep. Putting my cigarette out against the steel frame, I composed myself and walked around the corner. Again, I didn't want my aunt or uncle to give me a lecture about smoking.

A pair of brown leather boots and black jeans stuck out from underneath a car parked in the shop. The individual was struggling with something underneath the vehicle. I cleared my throat and heard the person put down the tools. It was obviously my aunt.

As the figure rolled out from underneath the car, I let out a gasp. It was not my aunt! It wasn't even a person, although it was shaped like a person with eyes, a nose, ears, and hands. It looked like a bronze robot—but not a robot. It had no wires, and I could see through it. Mechanical gears swirled inside. Locking, switching, and rotating. Was I dreaming or hallucinating? At the moment, I didn't care—it seemed too real. This creature stood up, walked toward me, and looked me in the eyes. I looked back into its metallic, concave surfaces that replaced the location of its irises. I didn't physically shake like at the hospital, but dread filled my heart.

"Who are you, and what are you doing here?" the thing asked and clicked.

"You can talk?" I responded automatically.

"Of course, boy! . . . And now *YOU* will talk." It picked up a wrench from the floor. I clutched my bow and arrows closer, forgetting I had them in my hands.

Again, I automatically asked, "What are you?"

"Hey boy, get a grip—I'm asking you a question! Who are you, and what are you doing here? You better tell me something soon, or I'll fetch the rifle or the phone, and there is no guarantee that I'm going for the phone." This creature raised its voice and pointed to the wall of the shop.

Standing in the doorway, dumbstruck, I answered the truth: "I'm Edward, and I'm staying here with my aunt and uncle because my mom is sick."

"Do you live here now?" the mechanical man asked and waved his wrench in the air.

"Yes, sir." I broke eye contact to look down at my mud-covered shoes for a second.

"Hmm." I looked back up to see bronze and silver gears turning behind his eyes, and I wondered what he was thinking. Why was he here? How did he work, and how was this possible? Was I just imagining him?

"Very well. In that case, take a seat, I insist." The creature waved his hand toward an old cloth office chair at a workbench. He lay back onto the creeper and slid back under the car. This made me feel a little easier, although I was still uncomfortable. I heard him working on the car's underside, letting off a swear and wrestling with something. I looked between his pant leg and shoe and noticed a round metallic joint with springs and widgets attached to a significant bearing. Is he all machine? Is there any human to him at all? Who made him?

"So now you know my name, who are you?" I demanded as I stood at the entrance and refused to take a seat.

"I bet you want to ask '*what* are you?' first," the machine grunted. "Well, I'll answer both—I'm an automaton. A mechanical robot-person." He stuck a large wrench out from underneath the car and waved it at me before pulling it back. "Not electric, and thank goodness for that. None of this modern crap. Technology makes us lazy." He banged on something, which caused the car to shift forward and backward. Silence filled the air for a couple of minutes. "My name is Mr. Chorales," he said in a raspy voice.

I sat still for a moment. I shivered a little, and the Automaton clanged and ticked, both with the car and inside his own body.

"I guess . . . Are . . . are you real?" I asked with feelings of sincerity.

"Definitely not. Are you real?" he responded. I was

momentarily relieved and then confused.

"Of course I'm real—I'm a person," I stammered.

"Just because you're a person doesn't mean that you are real. A rock is real, and it's not a person. Further, you could simply be a member of someone else's dream. You probably are. Why are you who you are when you could have been something else? You could have been a vat of butter, a mirror, or a dragonfly."

I didn't think of these questions; I couldn't. A small black rubber hose fell under the car and rolled near the garbage can.

"Toss that hose in that bin, we can't let things become a mess."

This automaton didn't seem interested in me at all. However, I was fascinated. As fear retracted, I was filled with curiosity.

"Mr. Chorales? What are you working on?"

"Just replacing a CV axle. This boot gave me grief—both of them." He cackled, pulled out from under the car, and sat on his creeper. He pulled up a sleeve and twisted his wrist around, clicking. "I gotta get both fixed."

"You break down?" I asked.

"Of course, everyone does. We all have sand in our joints and are trying to make it as far as possible before the desert buries us." He waved a copper finger around the room. "You ain't permanent, and thank God for that."

"Are you just in my head?" I changed the conversation.

"Yes, of course, and so are you," he responded, wiping off some tools with a rag. He then turned around in the darkness and disappeared. Same with the tools and the light. Suddenly I was standing in the workshop by myself, holding my bow and arrows in my odd, borrowed outfit from Adam's dresser. I felt sick with a buzzing in my head, and I shivered.

I slowly got up and made my way to the farmhouse. I could see the outside light glow with an orange tint while five small black flies whirled around it. It reminded me of ships to a lighthouse. My aunt was sleeping in the rocking chair in the living room. A stack of books was beside her. She woke up as I snuck past the screen door.

She looked shocked for a second and looked me up and down.

"I see you changed clothes and got something new?" She gestured to my arrows. She gave a gentle smile, yawned, and rubbed her eyes. "Fashionable." She pointed to the lines on my borrowed t-shirt.

Do I tell her about my experience at the workshop? Do I talk to her about Mr. Chorales? I didn't think so. She would feel that I was messed up. She would probably put me in the hospital. I wondered what I would see there. I decide not to say anything.

"Oh yeah, I slipped in some mud and fell down a hill, so Adam lent me some clothes to wear for the day. And Adam's dad gave me this bow. I think he wants me to practice with it because the whole family does archery."

Aunt Emma sighed. "The whole family did archery—not anymore. Ethan called to tell me that you went to the hospital to see Leah. She's a good girl. What did you think?"

I glanced away from the living room to look at the kitchen. I felt a deep wave welling in my chest. Deciding to give up, I hung my bow on the coat hanger and put on my hoodie. Pulling up the hood, I sat down and began sobbing. I hadn't cried in front of another person for a long time. I certainly hadn't planned on breaking down tonight. I heaved uncontrollably with pity for someone who I knew nothing about. The whole time, I didn't look up at my aunt to see the look on her face. She was probably disgusted.

*Clunk.* A box of tissues was placed on the TV tray beside me. I still didn't look up. I held my knees to my chest and wished I could be home. Not back in the city. Not even the bungalow when Dad was still alive. A different type of home. After no more tears arrived, I slowly looked up, disgusted with myself and my loss of control. Aunt Emma was sitting in the chair with a cup of tea in her hands, smiling gently. I didn't understand . . . I didn't even know what had happened. I was confused and lonely. Was I that upset about Leah? What was wrong?

"Do you want to talk?" Aunt Emma asked.

"No. I'm going to bed," I responded.

Later that night, I stuck my head out the window to have a cigarette. I could not sleep anyway. I wished for a drink as well. What is wrong with me? What is wrong with the world? Why are there sick kids? What did they do to deserve death? They don't even know what life is. I wish I could trade my life for hers. At least she's got a family.

Suddenly a memory grasped my attention. I remembered sitting in my mother's car. We were parked outside of the hospital back home. I had the choice to see Dad as he died, but I didn't want to. So I sat alone for an hour while the rest of my family was in the hospital. I should have been there. I could have done something. The horrors of my father's passing filled my imagination while I sat alone.

Again, I watched the breeze push the window curtains inward and outward like the breathing of the night sky. I felt like giving up. There's no controlling suffering . . . and who is Mr. Chorales? I looked out of the window and nearly jumped out of my skin. I saw two eyes looking right back at me through the frame. Two yellowish-green full moons peered into my own eyes. I wanted to get up and close the window, but I was too afraid to move. I thought of Adam's father's advice about animals with fangs in the woods. The eyes came closer and closer and finally sat on the windowsill. It was a cat! A black cat curiously bobbed its head toward me. It jumped down onto my floor and up on my bed. I didn't know what the rules were for cats. Were cats allowed in the house? They shouldn't be allowed on the bed. I guess it's better to ask forgiveness than permission, I thought. I just sat upright in my bed and scratched the cat's cheek. A deep purr built up inside it, lying at the foot of my bed. It gently closed its eyes and did a slow double blink toward me. The cat slept at the foot of my bed that night, but it was gone in the morning.

# Chapter 6

I stayed around the farm for the next few days doing chores and practicing archery with Adam. He came around every day after his morning work and regularly brought us some fruit and honey. I never had honey quite like this. It was chunky and flavorful, not just like sugar, but you could taste the fruit. I reminded myself that most of my food was from the land I lived on. I didn't tell anyone about my time with the Automaton, the cat, or my addictive habits. I felt like an imposter, unable to fit in. The people here were weird. One morning, I saw my aunt and uncle outside as the sun rose. They were digging fenceposts in their slippers and pink bathrobes. They seemed to know everything about everyone and kept talking about things and places I didn't know. I wasn't looking forward to the school year.

One day, Aunt Emma took me back to the hospital. We

sat in the parking lot. The farm truck was turned off, and I fidgeted with a water bottle while my aunt spoke. Her words seemed rehearsed and carefully selected.

"Edward, I want you to have lots of options and get you set up with something before school starts. This summer has been stressful, but I don't want you to feel alone. I know you can't talk to us about everything, so your uncle and I want you to see a psychologist."

I just stared at the heat waves distorting the painted lines of the parking lot as she spoke, avoiding eye contact.

"Psychologist? There's nothing wrong with me." I spat words out in defensiveness and maintained my gaze.

"I didn't say there was. You just had a rough couple of years, and I think it's about time to do something," my aunt gently stated.

"I've been doing stuff. I'm better off than Mom or my sister." I raised my voice. I was still on edge and stared off into the distance. I dug my fingernails into the truck seat.

"Your mom and sister aren't here; you are. I'm not taking care of your mom or sister; I'm taking care of you. Please go in." Her gentle tone began to flow harsher.

"Maybe," I said warily. As soon as I heard we were going to the hospital again, my stomach turned into knots, my legs when weak, and I felt sick. I also wondered about Leah—would she see me? I didn't really want to see her, although I knew it would be good for her to see people. I stepped out of the truck and locked the door from the inside before closing it. The last time I was at a hospital, it was not good. It had never been good.

Somehow I made it up the ramp and through the doors. There was the same reception area around the hospital entrance, and I noticed Aunt Emma leaning on the receptionist's counter, talking to someone behind it. They were laughing.

There was a single person in the reception area. It was the same old man. The one who had barged past me. He wore the same brown suit and black tie. He was turning his umbrella over in his hands.

"I'm late . . . I'm late," he muttered to himself.

"Hey, there." Aunt Emma took me by the shoulder and pointed me down a hallway. We followed a solid red line through a different hospital section this time. The walls turned from painted white plaster to a faded pink. When they changed colour, I noticed other changes. While one side of the hospital was clean and perfect, this side was getting dirtier and older with each step. Light bulbs were burnt out, and there were tiny lines of dirt on the edges of the hallway.

"Institutionalized," I said under my breath so my aunt couldn't hear me.

At last, we came to the end of the hallway as indicated by the end of the red line. A guard sat behind a window in a small room. He was reading a book: *One Hundred and One Parenting Tips*. He looked up with bloodshot eyes and a droopy face. He seemed to move with very little enthusiasm.

"Ah . . . we have an appointment . . . with Dr. Winters?" Aunt Emma stammered.

"Edward Lancer?" he asked with an emotionless face.

"Yes, sir," Aunt Emma responded. "That's us."

"All righty then, go on in and take the first door on your right." He buzzed the door, and a light above the door switched from a barely visible red to a bright green. Upon going through, I saw that the guard's small room extended to the other side of the locked doors.

*Click.* The doors locked behind us. It felt like a jail. It was a jail. We were standing in a large, rectangular room covered in the same dulled pink established in the previous hallway. To my left was a padded room. The entrance to the room was wide open. A man wearing pyjamas was sprawled out like a starfish in front of the door. He sang an indistinguishable song. The middle of the room hosted a large desk where three nurses sat; behind this, a tiny office with four large windows. Inside that office, a man in a dark green shirt sat with his back to us, typing notes on a computer. Around the room, there were tables and chairs scattered about with people sitting in them. One lady was pacing nervously back and forth while another man followed her saying nothing. A small child came up close to me and smiled—this was incredibly discomforting. I knew he couldn't do me much harm; after all, he was a lot smaller than me, but what happened to him? Why was he here? And why me?

Two old men were arguing at one table. One of the men

stood up and threw cards into the air, and they fluttered down to the floor like chickadees. This outburst caused the pacing woman to jump on one leg and yell, "Not me, not me." The nurses, all disinterested in the unusual action of the room, shuffled through their papers. Once we trundled toward the desk, all three looked up at me, Aunt Emma, and the smiling boy approaching. I turned my body away from the boy, but he grabbed my arm and held my hand. All three nurses were clothed in the same grey scrubs and shared many characteristics: glasses, age, and blank expressions. They shared a single magnifying glass, passing it to-and-fro with minimal communication.

"Steven, let go," one of the nurses yelled sternly at the boy. He started to sob and ran into the padded room, hugging himself while collapsing on the floor.

My aunt piped up, "Oh! The guard said . . ." A nurse pointed to the open door on the right.

"Go ahead." One of the nurses gestured and then looked down at her stack of papers.

As we walked to the room, we heard the wails of the boy and the screeching of "not me."

When we went into the room on the right, there was an ancient coffee table, two small yellow chairs, and one polished, oversized black leather chair. Two foldable chairs were tucked in by the window. This window had five thick metal bars on it. While the room appeared aged, the black chair and the bars seemed very well kept.

"Well . . . I guess we are here," Aunt Emma said as she pulled the door shut. I looked between the chairs and picked the one farthest away from the fancy leather one. Aunt Emma sat in the other yellow chair. We sat in silence for a while, and then she began to speak.

"I'm sorry. I—"

She was cut off by the quick opening of the door. A short, lean man walked in. He must have been about thirty-five with blond hair and dark brown eyes. He was the one that was wearing the green shirt and typing on the computer. He cleared his throat and sat down. Triple clicking his pen, he opened a black binder and flipped to the middle.

"Who are you?" He gestured with his hand broadly to Aunt Emma and me without looking at us.

"Well, I'm Emma, and this is my nephew, Edward."

"Are you his legal guardian?"

"Yes, his mother was—"

"I'm sorry, but I'll get to that when it's time." He aggressively flipped his paper over and looked at his watch. He then wrote something on the top of his form.

"Do you go by Edward or Ed?"

"Edward."

"Ok, so why are you here?" He looked at my aunt, who gestured to me. "Please, I'd like to hear from you first." He insisted on my aunt speaking.

"Before I start, are you Dr. Winters?" she questioned with a furrowed brow.

"No, I'm Dr. Nialliv; Dr. Winters is not here yet. She is a recent hire, and I will be completing your intake interview for her. She was supposed to start this week but broke her leg and won't come in until next week. Is that ok?" he asked, making direct eye contact with my aunt.

"I suppose it is, as long as we see her." At this point, Aunt Emma seemed confrontational.

"Don't worry," he responded coolly. "Ok, so what's the problem?" Again, he was looking at my aunt and ignoring me.

"Well, I don't know where to start."

"Just start anywhere; I'm very good at piecing things together," he said boastfully, writing notes down on his paper. I didn't know what he was possibly writing; we hadn't said anything yet.

"Edward used to live with his parents in the city. About two years ago, Edward's father died in a warehouse accident. Edward and his older sister Tabitha are the two kids; she is now twenty-one years old. Edward's mother—oh, my husband's sister—took the death hard. The whole family did. They had to sell the house because Edward's mother could not work, and they moved into a small apartment. I think the space was too cramped for Tabitha, so she moved about one hour away from the city and works at a restaurant. She has some problems too." I stared at a white floor tile, holding back tears and anger.

My aunt continued. "I think Edward's mother may have

started drinking more and gambled at the casino with the money she got from insurance and the settlement. I'm sure Edward looked after her when someone called children's protection."

"Do you know who?" Dr. Nialliv asked.

"Maybe a neighbour? He wasn't going to school."

"Hmm . . ." With a pause and a smile, he responded, "So, what are you looking for here?" He continued to look at my aunt.

She looked at me as she responded. "I think you should ask Edward that. I think that it would be nice to talk to a professional about the large life changes and his father passing away. It would help with school and to get some direction for the future."

"I see. I'm sure Dr. Winters would be up for that. Usually, we do six to eight sessions for an issue like that, including this one." Finally turning to me, he asked, "Ok, Edward, what do you want?"

"I don't know," I responded, still looking down. I didn't like the guy; I actually hated him. Who was he? What gave him the right?

The doctor filled in our awkward pause. "I know that when we are not adults, it's difficult to know what's best, that's why I would like to do an intake assessment. I want you to answer these on a scale of one to five."

For the rest of the session, Dr. Nialliv went through three assessments until the hour was completed. One time during a question, a high-pitched shriek came from underneath the door, and he just kicked the door near the bottom. When the shrieker laughed uncontrollably, the doctor got up, adjusted his tie, and swiftly went outside. There was a series of metallic clicks and a slam. The doctor returned and straightened out his hair and tie; both were out of order upon his re-entry. Soon after, he finished the tests and added up the scores. I was as honest as possible, although I didn't trust Nialliv.

"Edward, have you wondered about what you're seeing? Maybe you see things that aren't there?"

I thought back to Mr. Chorales, the Automaton. "Never," I answered.

"Ok, have you noticed any life changes since everything started to happen?"

Of course I had. I'd started drinking and smoking, we stopped going out, we cut all communication from family, Mom gambled, Tabitha abandoned me, I dropped out of school, and I fantasized about running away.

"Nope," I responded.

"I guess that's it for today. Dr. Winters will see you at the same time next week. Goodbye." Dr. Nialliv picked up his papers while accidentally leaving one. After he left, I leaned forward and saw that it was a list of prescriptions and people's names attached. Should I pick it up and try to give it back to him? No. I just left it where it was.

As Aunt Emma and I got back into the truck, she put her head down on the steering wheel, sighed, and smiled as she turned to look at me. "I won't blame you if you don't want to go back . . . I wouldn't." That was all that she said as we drove back home. I had lots to say, but nothing came out. Again, I felt the longing to go back home—not to the farm, but my real home where Dad would take me biking, Tabitha would play the trumpet, and my mom would be a mother.

# Chapter 7

Adam's dad drove us to the first day of school. I hadn't experienced the first day of school in two years, and I was definitely not looking forward to it. After all, what was the point? I was just going to get a job working with my hands anyways. That was what all the other teachers had said about me. I didn't need to learn anything from this school; it was just a factory that created obedient, brainwashed workers.

Again, we pulled up to the dusty schoolyard. The students arrived via diesel trucks, dirt bikes, bicycles, long cars, and even horses. The parking lot was three-quarters filled this time; it seemed that most students were already inside the school. A couple of students were standing outside, talking to each other. They didn't care as much about their looks as people back home. They seemed to all dress in the same way, regardless of gender. Jeans and a t-shirt. I also noticed a younger student throwing lawn darts at one of the pine trees.

"Wow! The parking lot is absolutely packed!" Adam exclaimed. He excitedly tapped his cowboy boots on the truck's floor and wrung his hands together. I could see him in the side of the mirror.

"Hey! There's Bill—I'll introduce you. He's the captain of the wrestling team." I sighed as I grabbed my backpack and mentally prepared myself.

Adam and I jumped out of the truck and started to head toward one of the groups of students. "Heya, Bill. How's your summer?" Before Bill had a chance to respond, Adam interjected. "Edward, this is Bill, and Bill, this is Edward. I was just telling him that you're the team's captain."

We shook hands, and I could tell that Adam idolized Bill. I'm not entirely sure why. If I were to pass him on the street or see him in the halls, I wouldn't think twice about stopping to talk to him. He was perhaps the most ordinary-looking person I had seen. He had brown hair and dull brown eyes and seemed to painfully wince his eyes shut with every blink.

"P-p-p-plea-eased to mmmmmeet you," he stammered. Bill didn't say much. Probably because it took so much effort to say anything. He just smiled and then looked down, rolling a rock on the ground with the toe of his runner.

While others talked, I just smiled and allowed Adam to do all the speaking. That kid could talk about anything for days. Everyone seemed to know it too. It wasn't as if people avoided Adam; however, they seemed to understand just how to manage his excitement about life.

"Welcome to your last first day. Except you, Nick, you'll be here for another three years," the teacher teased a large student in the front row. The student picked something out of his backpack and tossed it to the teacher; it was a pineapple covered in writing. The teacher read the message, chuckled to himself, and launched the pineapple back.

"Well, there's always something new around here." The teacher wrote his name and the date on the board: *September 3, 1995. Mr. Letvine.* While taking attendance, he stopped at two names—the first mine and another student named Jason—and welcomed us. He already knew the other kids from other years because he had taught them before. This reminded me of how small the school was. It also reminded me that I probably stuck out among these kids that knew each other.

"Edward and Jason, please go to the office and sign up for your classes. I don't think you'll miss too much while you are gone."

While Mr. Letvine said this, he pulled out a green bin from underneath his desk and brought it up to the front. Then he began distributing tennis balls to the front row.

Jason and I walked down the hallway. It was still dim in the school despite the humming fluorescent lights. Even though kids had trampled through in the morning, the wavey tiled floor was still perfectly waxed.

"What a joke of a school. Actually, forget the school—what

a joke of a town. These people are nuts. Where did you come from?" Jason's words echoed down the hall as he looked around disgustedly. He sneered at the floor, walls, and ceiling. He stepped higher than necessary as we walked, avoiding the ground as if the tile was mud.

At this point, I got a strange feeling about Jason. He was wearing a golf shirt and khaki pants with semiformal black shoes, hardly fitting into the rural fashion exhibited by the other kids. He talked a little differently. I didn't want to give him more information than he was asking. "I'm from Edmonton."

"Oh yes, I know where that is. I'm from Seattle, Washington. My father owned a shipping company, and when he got divorced from my mom, he sold it all and moved here. He wants to build a ski resort here. Do these people even know what skis are?"

"Yeah," I said absent-mindedly. I was already tuned out of the conversation.

"The drunk idiot," Jason muttered under his breath. "Anyways, I wonder if there are any options worth signing up for. My last school was private; we had over twenty different classes to choose from."

We arrived at the office. The door was open, and a very tall and slender lady sat at the receptionist's desk. Upon arrival, she looked up and gestured to a room behind her. She didn't ask for our names but said, "Good to see you, Edward and Jason."

Sitting down at a round wooden table in a small room, Jason hissed, "How do you think she knew our names?" It was apparent that this area was also used as a sick room. A small bed sat across us, and some medical supplies lined the shelf beside the table.

"Ok! I'll be right there." A coarse male voice came from the main office room. The owner of the voice walked in. He was a short man shaped like an ice cream cone and sported a brown suit. "I'm your principal, and I would like to get you boys signed up for classes. We have decided to allow all grades to attend option classes. This means that you will be attending classes with younger students."

Jason exhaled loudly and rolled his eyes. The principal frowned at Jason and continued. "With that in mind, the teachers will do their best to accommodate your skill level. Here are your signup sheets. Math, science, language, and social are not optional—you will take two of these each half of the year, and you get to choose four options total."

I looked through the six options: resourcefulness, woodwork, metalwork, food, music, and gym.

"What is resourcefulness?" I asked.

"Yes, I guess we need to change that name. It's our most popular class. It's a class where you learn about survival and skills that aren't commonly used today. Normally we wouldn't give you all these options, but we would like to give both of you more opportunities because you will only be here for a year before you graduate." He spoke in a proud tone.

"Resourcefulness and gym?" I asked Jason with my eyebrows slightly lifted. "And then metalwork and foods?"

"I guess," Jason responded, clearly frustrated that he wouldn't have the same experience as his last school.

"Ok, here you go, here's your schedule." The principal handwrote our timetables down and handed them to us. "I hope you enjoy your year."

For the rest of the day, I stayed by Jason. It only seemed natural. His cynicism was predictable and unchanging. Since we were in the same classes every now and then, Bill would check in on me.

I ate a sandwich from Aunt Emma during lunch and talked to Adam. He and Bill exchanged wrestling strategies and sports statistics. After that, some other students came over and chatted about dirt bikes. I knew nothing about the subject, not just dirt bikes, but everything discussed throughout the day. Since I'd missed the past two school grades, I just sat there, not following the teacher's instructions. I just daydreamed and looked at textbook pictures while the teacher spoke. This year would be about surviving, then I would find a job and get out of here.

At the end of the first day, I walked to my uncle's metalworking shop.

"Well, how was it?" my uncle asked through bites of a donut. Sparks, smoke, and testosterone flew through the air.

"I'm stupid, and I won't be able to catch up. But I'll graduate."

My uncle stopped chewing and looked at me. "That's a spirit—maybe not *the* spirit, but that will work."

I was a little surprised by his response. After allowing him to finish his donut, I asked, "Hey, I know this year will go by fast, and today I was thinking of what comes after. Do you think I could work for you? I mean, here at the shop instead of chores on the farm?"

Uncle Matt grunted. "To be honest, I see a lot of work coming our way very soon. I'm working with a new customer building a massive project. He just moved here."

"A ski hill?" I questioned.

"Yeah—wait, how did you know?"

"I go to school with his son."

"He has a son? I would have never thought of him as a father. Maybe keep that to yourself: the ski hill, not the son. I don't know if we will get the contract to assemble everything. I just don't want to count my chicks before they are hatched. I could expand my business threefold if everything goes through, I would need to." He gave a distant chuckle, and I could almost see dollar signs glaze across his eyes.

"Well, could you let me know if something happens, and I could work a little? There's not much going on in my life right now," I lied and secretly thought of all the catching up required to graduate.

"Well, I'll talk to Emma, but I bet you could help us. Maybe just on Mondays, Tuesdays, and Wednesdays. A lot of our work will be off-site, and there won't be anyone here."

"Thanks, that will help me a lot."

While I waited for Uncle Matt to finish his paperwork, I did something unusual. I grabbed a dustpan and broom and began to clean. I didn't tell him that I was planning to save the money to get out of the town and return to the city when I graduated. I figured that if I could convince him that I was a good worker, he would have no choice but to hire me.

We drove home, and he picked up hamburgers for us. While we were sitting in the drive-through, I pointed. "What's that building? It looks so weird." Across from the drive-through sat an octagonal building with a tall roof, almost a steeple. It had windows looking out in every direction and was impeccably kept. The outside stucco was a soft white, and a brick pathway circled the building. The roof was ageing; the shingles were beginning to bend upward.

"Oh, that's our church."

"Cherry Lake has a church? That looks pretty fancy."

"Yeah, I guess three congregations decided to share the same building. I guess it makes more sense financially. One of the pastors is nasty, though, a real piece of work. I don't understand why someone who hates people would choose to work with them." Uncle Matt snickered.

He always seemed to enjoy irony and bizarre experiences. At least that was my conclusion after our regular talks about bigfoot, aliens, hidden treasure, and secret government organizations. Although these topics were interesting and exciting, the genuinely bizarre conversations surrounded people.

Nothing changed throughout the week. I attended my core classes, and my uncle got me started on small jobs around the shop. Every day I smoked from the school to the train tracks and then dragged my feet the rest of the way, thinking and worrying. I dreaded my upcoming appointment with my new psychologist. Uncle Matt got the contract for the ski hill and took me there after school one day. He showed me the premade metal pieces used in the gondola. I couldn't believe that I was part of creating this project.

\*

"This town is an absolute dump and a waste of space," Jason snarled. We were walking around the town one afternoon after school. Up and down the back roads, kicking rocks, drinking pop, and eating stolen crab apples. "Dad is always busy; there's nothing good to do here. He doesn't even need the money. I don't understand why I have to be here," he repeated. Jason's rants were constant, predictable, and spiteful. I could allow my mind to wander and miss nothing new, so that was what I did. I suddenly became aware that Jason had stopped talking and walking beside me. He was looking into a backyard.

Jason piped up, peering over the fence, "Hey, look at that!"

I joined him at the fence and looked over. There was a long backyard with a clothesline draped from the alley to the house. It was covered in pyjamas, although that was not what we were looking at. An emu stood in the middle of the yard, picking at an orange bin. We looked at each other and looked back. Yes, it was a genuine emu, in the middle of the town. It was the last place one would expect to see an emu—at a small pink house with a white picket fence. The entire property had the 1960s "American Dream" vibe. Meanwhile, the emu appeared scrappy and twitchy, pecking at the bin.

"Well, that's unexpected. Here, hold my legs." Jason started to climb up the fence.

"What are you doing? Don't go up there, you'll get us into trouble," I hissed.

"Just watch," Jason sneered and grabbed one side of the clothesline and rotated it toward him, bringing the bedsheets closer. "Here, take this." He threw a white sheet over his back and it floated down to the gravel. I didn't want any part of this. Jason laid out the bedsheet and folded it over again and again. Once it was a long rectangle, he began twisting and turning. I still didn't know what he was making, but once I saw the result, I was thrilled.

"Ta-dah!" He held up an oversized tie. "Now, time for our good friend to have some style. Take your finger and scratch underneath the fence. Once the emu looks down, I'll climb up and whistle. When I whistle, you stop, the emu will look up, and I'll toss this around his neck."

I had my doubts, but at this point, I just wanted to see it through. I didn't think the bird could possibly get hurt. We did exactly as Jason said, and before the emu knew, it was a significantly more formal bird. We knew better than to linger, so we rushed off, cackling and snorting in laughter down the alley. It was the first time I could remember Jason smiling. Soon after, his scowl returned.

# Chapter 8

"Ed—come down, please," my uncle bellowed up the farm stairs. I was in my bedroom trying to make sense of the homework the teacher assigned. The door was closed, and the mysterious black cat was again on my lap, purring. I shooed the cat onto the roof, shut the window, and headed downstairs, closing the door halfway shut. My aunt appeared nervous as she sat nearby in the living room chair. As I descended the stairs, I noticed a policeman standing in the front entranceway and frowning at me. He stood with his arms crossed. I looked at him and tried not to break eye contact as I moved toward the entrance. My mind spiralled into a series of accusations and suspicions. Did he know what I had done with Jason? Did he know what had happened in Edmonton? Why was he here? Who had told on me?

"Are you Edward?" he demanded.

"Yes," I said with caution.

"Do you know anything about this?" He pulled a folded photograph from his back pocket. It was a picture of an emu by the highway. "Earlier today, this was reported. I have already talked to a neighbour, and they described two boys doing something suspicious around the back alley."

I looked over the photo of the emu—this one was without a tie. However, it did appear to have the same scrappy appearance. I just about answered with a lie, but then I waited and gave it some thought. I don't understand what overtook me, but instead of brushing off the truth, I told him what had happened.

"I don't want too much trouble for my aunt and uncle . . . and I'm not certain this is our emu. My friend and I were walking around this afternoon and saw the emu in a backyard. So I helped him over the fence, and we made a tie out of a bedsheet. Then we put it on him and walked away. We didn't let the emu out; I think that would be going too far. We wanted some fun, and we didn't mean any harm." I finished with a shrug.

The police officer frowned. "First of all, get better friends; secondly, I appreciate your honesty. Unfortunately, there will still need to be a punishment because laws were broken. We have proof that this was the same emu. Fortunately, we have a program here where you and your friend don't have to pay a fine or anything like that. I'm not in charge, but I think some community volunteer hours could clear things up."

"Yes, sir." I honestly didn't know what to say. I just looked down.

He continued, "I'm glad you told the truth because I just came from questioning your friend. It seems like he was reluctant to say anything."

Many thoughts went through my mind. Disappointment about volunteer service, shame about breaking trust with Jason, and some pride in coming clean.

"Thanks, officer, we will have a talk," my uncle spoke with a severe tone.

"Please phone this number between 9 a.m. and 5 p.m. so we can work something out." The officer handed a pamphlet to my uncle. I felt sick. I'd only been here two weeks and I'd messed things up. Again.

The officer left, stepping over the pig on the porch, and I was instructed to sit at the kitchen table. Uncle Matt and Aunt Emma left the house to talk in whispers in front of the steps. I tried to listen to them. The window was open, and there was a slight breeze. Still, they didn't talk loud enough for me to hear.

Coming in, my uncle sighed. "Ed, I understand wanting a bit of fun. Both your mother and I grew up on a farm where nothing happened. We made our own fun. Just how you went about it was not—"

I interrupted, "But I didn't—"

My uncle slammed his hand down on the table. It was like a firecracker going off indoors.

"Let me finish," he bellowed. His eyes pierced me, and I felt a flame of anger. "I was saying that I think what you did was funny but not respectful and could have ended up with a dead bird or a traffic accident. Did it ever occur that the emu could have accidentally hung itself? That bird is the property of a very old woman; she used to be a neighbour. When she was forced to move into town, she had to give up everything but the bird. I'm disappointed because we expected you to keep your head on straight after this second chance at a normal life."

I waited for a minute before saying, "Yes, sir."

My aunt started to speak, "Edward, you need to realize that this is a small community. Honour and image mean something here. If you mess up and make a mistake, these people are quick to judge and forgive, but they have difficulty with trust. They may see you as a 'vandal' or 'irresponsible kid.' Honour is worth more than money—it is your golden ticket. I expect more from you."

I didn't have much to say. I just nodded my head and walked up to my bedroom to finish my studies and go to sleep. Oddly enough, I didn't have trouble falling asleep. I'd finally gotten caught, but I accepted the consequences: walking on my own terms. It made me feel more like a man and less like a boy.

I tried to tell Adam this the next day. We were on our way to look at comics at New-to-You, a secondhand store that sold a plethora of junk. The store's sign was painted on an old surfboard and hung just above the door by a yellow rope. A porch wrapped the entire outside of the store paired with worn cedar siding.

Opening the door with a creak, Adam and I turned to the right and saw an old man sleeping with a comic book resting on his lap. Deeply breathing, he seemed to be part of his collection. A person who had made himself truly embedded with his work. I had seen him many times before: the crooked nose, reading glasses, tilted back baseball cap. The store owner. Not wanting to wake him, I took my first step into the shop. *Creak!* The floorboard groaned and startled the man from his nap. Jumping up while dropping his comic, he looked around in a panic and automatically cleaned the counter as if we were to convict him of slothfulness.

"Do you need any help?" the owner asked with flared nostrils and wide eyes.

"No, sir, I think I know where to look."

"Ok, just let me know if you need anything." He picked up his comic book and sat back down.

"Thanks," we both responded.

The store's main level was filled with items that could be sold quickly: an old canoe, snowshoes, and a poorly made taxidermy duck among recognizable and unrecognizable junk. Downstairs an old bulb flickered with cobwebs clinging to it; I cautiously grabbed the rail as I walked down the stairs. As the handrail wobbled, I gave up on it and hoped the stairs would hold me. They creaked, threatening to buckle with every step. Comics were absolutely packed in. Aren't we a bit old for children's stories? I wondered. We stood side by side, flipping through the selection.

I told Adam everything: the emu, the police officer, and the feeling of satisfaction when I confronted my actions. What I thought about nearly killing the bird.

"I get it," Adam responded solemnly.

I was shocked. "You don't seem to be the kind of guy to get in trouble."

"I don't think it's about getting in trouble; it's getting yourself in gear and making the most with what you got. My parents were strict with us growing up. If they weren't, sheep would die and fruit would rot. I suppose that's why little Leah can fight so hard."

"How did it happen? What happened?" I asked.

"With what? Leah getting sick? I guess she was just always sick and in pain. I don't know why, but the doctors said it was highly treatable, yet here we are. Maybe there is something else going on, I don't know."

I was surprised that Adam was able to talk so openly about this. I hadn't told him about my mom or sister, nor had he asked. I think he didn't need to ask. We found about three different bags of books during the remainder of our comic book hunting. These small collections were dirt cheap. In addition to the comics, I found an old record player by a series of encyclopedias. This came with three records of my choice and headphones for thirty dollars. I used to listen to music back home, but it had been either silence, animals, or farm machinery since I'd arrived at Cherry Lake.

Adam's dad was filling up his truck at the gas station beside the secondhand store. Walking between the manual pumps, I noticed that the gas price was seventy-one cents a gallon—a low price. Of course it was; nothing ever changed here. Even though it had never been updated, it appeared to never age.

"What's with the price?" I asked as I walked into the store. The gas attendant didn't even look up from his fishing magazine. He shifted his weight on his stool and picked his teeth with a toothpick.

"It's been broken since 1972. Why, do you want to buy some gas?" he muttered as he sipped a beer.

"Nah, just wondering about the pumps."

"Well, if there is something that you want to buy, let me know."

I couldn't see much in the gas station—what little was there appeared forcefully random. A box of lemons, train spikes, firewood, and a sack of marbles were already placed on the counter. There were blueberry bagels for sale inside of a clear bread box. Peering closer to them, I noticed a blueberry moving. Then the tiny blueberry looked up at me and scuttled away in a crab-like fashion. I don't know what it was, but it looked like a beetle or ant. A blueberry-eating ant.

"Hey buddy, you have bugs in your bagels." I beckoned to the attendant.

"Hmm," the gas attendant groaned.

I bought a cigar, some cigarettes, and a new lighter.

Adam and I sat in the back of the truck, leaned up against the back window, and drank pop with nectarines that hadn't managed to sell at the farmer's market. The sun was beginning to set as Adam's father dropped me off at the driveway to my aunt and uncle's farm. Chuckling to myself, I made my way up the driveway to the immovable red gate.

Preparing to duck through it, I hear a rustle and a voice.

"Missing this?"

I was shocked at what I saw: the Automaton stepping out from behind a tree.

"Mr. Chorales?"

He walked as if his joints didn't match each step, and his legs were mixed up. He almost fell into a stumble and rattled as he did so. He sauntered close to me with my wallet in his hands.

# Chapter 9

"I didn't think you were coming back," I responded in shock.

"I never left; I'm always around here. I work here," Mr. Chorales responded in a rough voice.

"But you're not really here, are you?"

"What proof do you need?"

I looked into his mechanical eyes and decided that this must be a hallucination, some type of dream. Surely this can't be real. Yet he was standing here. I reached out my hand, and he shook it. His cold mechanical hand was firm.

"Pleased to meet you. What do you need from me?" the Automaton asked bluntly.

"What can you offer?" I asked, mirroring his directness.

He cracked half a smile. "That's the first real question you have asked. I guess I can give many things. Let's start with this: you may know what smart people say or think, but true intelligence or wisdom is shown through the questions we ask. Try it."

"What question should I ask?" I respond, confused.

"Excellent start," he replied hoarsely. I remained puzzled.

"Umm . . . Why did I feel good when I told the police officer the truth?"

"I think you know the answer to that one. But this time, let's get a better answer—and the better answer comes with a better question. Start by replacing 'why' with 'what is the reason' and become more descriptive. You have a brain—use it."

I needed to think for several moments before constructing a sentence that beautifully and perfectly illustrated my curiosity.

"What is the reason behind feeling shame?"

"That's it!" The Automaton pointed at me and jumped about.

"Hey," I pondered, "how can you teach me something if you're just in my head?"

"Ah, we are going for two questions. You tell me the answer."

Again, I needed to pause. "The reason for feeling shame is learning how to act next time. As for the second question, you can teach me to think because I already knew how to."

"Are those true?" he asked, his eyes widening, ticking, and clicking.

"I don't feel like it . . . But . . . I think that they are the best I will get right now. Hey—how come you're interested in helping me?" I asked.

"I'm not just helping you, we are helping us, that's the point of conversation."

"I guess I haven't had many conversations," I replied.

"No, we certainly have not."

At this, Mr. Chorales lit up a cigar and walked past an old pine tree. As he moved toward the back of the tree, he became less visible; however, past the halfway mark, the fiery glow from the cigar rapidly accelerated quickly, causing a blazing flash that cloaked the entire clockwork creature in a fire. Then he was gone. For a couple of seconds, I stood there in shock. Then, after becoming aware of my environment and situation, I shook my head and made my way to the farmhouse.

I rested in bed that night listening to my new records and thinking about the Automaton. Who is he? What is he? Why is he so interested in helping me find questions? Don't I know everything that I need to know? Maybe I need to know something that no one else knows? My mind spiralled around in clumsy circles, like a kitten wrestling his own tail on the ground. Despite the chaos, I fell into a deep state of awareness. I didn't remember falling asleep.

I woke up in my dream, gasping for breath. I looked around me, and I was in a field—no hills, mountains, or valleys. Only a slight downward slope in all directions from where I was standing. Since I was on the precipice of this prairie land, I could see that there was no body of water—no lake, river, or ocean. Looking up at the sky, I saw no clouds, also with no end. The sky itself was removed from existence. I saw stars and galaxies that danced a ballet of creation and destruction. Darkness birthing light and then becoming consumed by an abyss of expansion. This lifting caused a great sensation of inner awareness. I felt like a canned sardine opened to the rest of reality.

I discovered that I was sinking only when I knew I was standing. If I hadn't become aware, I wouldn't have actually sunk. I didn't know how I knew this; the knowledge just popped into my mind. The soil crept upward, grasping at my ankles. This was similar to standing on a sandy beach and getting slowly sucked downward when the waves retreat. I began to panic as I was gradually swallowed by the earth, so I moved. Of course, the direction would be downhill, so I made my journey. In the dream, this continued for hours. I would sometimes stop and look around, but it was always the same scene. The ground would lap at my ankles threateningly, the sky was gone, and the earth was flat. I decided the best way to walk was to spiral slowly downward instead of abandoning the high point. I became exhausted in my dream, and as I turned my head to look up at the tallest point, I saw something. A golden pillar appeared out of nowhere, and a white peacock with brown speckles sat on top. It turned one of its eyes and looked at me.

At this, I woke up.

*

Jason ran toward me outside on the field during lunchtime. We were sitting in the shade of a lofty pine tree. I was with Adam, Bill, two girls, and another boy from grade eleven. As Jason approached, I noticed that he was mouthing something and fuming. He took a handful of dust from the ground and flung it into my eyes. Shocked, I stood up while Jason grabbed me by the collar, shoving me up to the chain-link fence. He shook me, and I didn't know what to do.

He screamed, "You sold me out? You jerk—no wonder your family didn't want you. You're a pathetic worm. Didn't you think about me? What my father would do?" His voice wavered at that last sentence. He turned from anger to sadness and back to fury. He then looked down and spat at my shoes.

I felt something swelling in my body. Jason continued to hold me against the fence and yell, spit flew into my face and hair, but I just stood there. Grit from the dust caused my eyes to squint.

"Well—aren't you going to do anything?" He seemed even more frustrated now that he wasn't getting a response. I didn't have much to say. We did something stupid, and it was over; community service and everything would be fine. I guess Jason didn't see it that way. My complete lack of reaction seemed to be his snapping point. Reaching his hands up to my neck, he began to choke me. At first, I didn't realize what was happening because my brain wasn't processing what my eyes were seeing. I couldn't breathe, so I grabbed his wrists, but he pushed me back into the fence. As soon as his arms were raised, Bill started to get up. And just as quickly as Jason grabbed me, Bill grabbed Jason and flipped him onto the ground, turning and twisting him into a human pretzel. I dropped to my knees, gripping my neck, trying to breathe, but nothing was happening. Bill and Jason came to a halt, and Jason made no sounds. Bill, however, had a lot to say.

Without stuttering, he yelled, "DON'T YOU TOUCH HIM—I don't care what he did, but don't you touch him." Jason looked shocked at Bill's ability to speak freely and wrestled in his grasp. It was useless. Bill had about twenty-five pounds on Jason and was obviously highly experienced in wrestling.

I regained my breathing and looked around. I had landed on an anthill. A teacher ran toward us, and ants were biting at my wrists.

"Bill—let him go," a teacher commanded.

"Are y-y-you sure?" he asked, reverting back to his stutter.

"Yes," she responded sternly.

They separated us in the office, which was for the best. I was surprised they didn't call Jason's father or my relatives to come to the school. I guess things were done a little different here. The principal walked into my room, the same room we first met in, the nurse's office. I held an ice pack to my neck and bubbled in my anger.

# Chapter 10

"How's the neck?" the principal asked. He looked very serious and twitched his mustache side to side.

"Cold and miserable," I responded.

"Understandable . . . So, Jason told me a bit of what happened, but I would like to hear your side of the story. What would you like to say?"

I told him everything, from the emu to the police officer and Bill's rescue. Naturally, I left out all parts about the Automaton—no one needed to hear that. I also talked about confessing, although I felt rather sheepish about that.

"Hmm. That gives us lots to think about. Don't worry, you're not in trouble." He nodded and raised his eyebrows. "I don't know if Jason is controlling himself, so I will do what I can to keep you safe. We will get both of you to talk this through, but another day." He stopped and tapped his foot on the floor. "I heard that both of you have disciplinary action after school? At the courthouse?"

"Yes, sir," I responded, looking down at my feet.

"Ok, so I'm going to give you two choices; for the rest of the day, you can be in class or the library. Jason will be wherever you aren't."

"I think I would like to be back in class." The meeting was straight after school, and I was nervous and not looking forward to the results. I thought staying in the library would be more fun; however, I knew that anticipation of the courthouse would make the day draw long.

Opening the door to the math room, I quickly stepped inside and took my spot in the third row from the front. Bill patted me on the back as I moved past him. I gave him a smile of thanks. Some of the other classmates watched the door behind me but gave up after a few minutes when Jason didn't follow. I don't think they were too disappointed—after all, they didn't seem to like him.

After school, my aunt and uncle were waiting in the parking lot. I nearly didn't recognize them as they were dressed in semi-formal wear. I looked at myself and wondered if I would be ok dressed like this: blue jeans and a black t-shirt. Oh—and was Jason around? I saw many faces rushing past, but no Jason. My mind startled as I remembered that he was free and could attack again at any moment.

A tingle of anger filled the air between my aunt, uncle, and me. I didn't tell them about what happened at school—now wasn't the time. I'd let them know after the meeting. We pulled up to the courthouse. This was the second street up from the lake. Old trees towered on both sides of the road and nearly touched leaves, causing the road to appear more like a tunnel. The courthouse was the same sandstone finish as the school and was shaped like a cube. There were hardly any windows outside. I began sweating.

As we pulled up, I hissed to my aunt and uncle, "Don't get out. That's Jason and his father."

Jason was folding papers and yelling something, and his father was trying to calm him down. Both were in suits—Jason must have changed. What was his punishment? What happened in there? After they left, we got out of the truck and approached the courthouse steps. Inside, the floor was a white stone, remarkably fancy for the town's size. A silver clock hung by the ceiling and whirled. It reminded me of the Automaton. As I approached the reception area, a lady asked, "Edward?"

"Yes, that's me," I responded.

She smiled and stood up to shake our hands. She took us down a long hallway and into a completely ordinary room. I'd expected a more eventful room. I was almost disappointed with the normality of the walls, the single round table, and foldable chairs. When I first thought of a courthouse, I thought of a grand courtroom filled with spectators and oak finishing. Perhaps a judge with a white wig. I ate a mint and wondered, Is this where everything will happen?

"Please take a seat. I'll let everyone know you are here."

After a couple of minutes, the same police officer came in with an older man. The older man had untamed white hair and was dressed in semiformal clothing. He was chuckling with the police officer as they walked. He also smiled at me. Why were people smiling here?

"So, Edward . . . and family . . . I'm glad that you're here. My name is Mr. Tofs, and I will be handling your case with Officer Smith. I run a program called the SYA, the Support Youth in Action group. We aren't interested in legal action but offer help to those under eighteen. Basically, we provide an opportunity for those who break the law to complete community service. However, this is completely voluntary; you will not get a better deal. This is a learning opportunity."

I decided that I could trust Mr. Tofs.

"I have worked with Officer Smith and legal counsel to suggest completing two seven-and-a-half-hour place-ments—one at the church and one at the hospital."

"The . . . the . . . hospital?" I respond, although not entirely aware that I was saying anything.

"Yes, sir. So, all together, only fifteen hours of community service. You can do it as quickly or as slowly as you want. You just need to get it done before the end of November. I will leave you three to talk." Mr. Tofs gestured to my aunt, uncle, and me.

As soon as they left the room, my aunt quietly spoke. "Edward, I think he's right; you're not going to get a better deal than this. You won't get anything on your record, and you will get community recognition." I looked at my uncle, and he just nodded.

"Ok," I sighed. I was not looking forward to this work; however, I needed to do it.

My aunt opened the door to invite the officer and Mr. Tofs back in. Then Aunt Emma gestured to me.

"Mr. Tofs, I think I'll do it," I declared.

"That was easier than the last boy." He looked back toward the officer and smirked. He pulled out a bundle of papers and got Aunt Emma and Uncle Matt to sign them. Finally, when it was time to go, he gave me a couple of sheets and a timesheet to be filled by my volunteer supervisors.

We got some fast food and dropped my uncle off at the workshop. Neither my aunt nor uncle said much, but I could tell they were relieved with my choice. Again, I was off to the hospital for my second appointment. I guess when it rains, it pours. I felt like this single day was taking me a lifetime to complete. I was exhausted and not looking forward to my session; I shared eye contact with my aunt, sighed, and exited the truck. Seeing Dr. Nialliv was the last thing that I wanted to do. I had promised Aunt Emma and myself that I would make a second effort. One more time. How much worse could this day get?

Opening the hospital door was slightly more manageable, and I didn't understand why. What had changed? It wasn't because I'd had a pleasant experience last time. I thought of the speckled peacock in my dream. The older man was asleep in his chair in the reception area. He wore the same suit and tie. An umbrella leaned against the bottom of his chair, and a small white teddy bear holding a heart was tucked in his suit jacket. He slept with his head back and seemed peaceful. His top dentures became loose in his mouth as he slept with his mouth cracked open. It was both disgusting and charming.

"Excuse me, are you Edward?" a middle-aged woman with a leg cast asked me. She didn't look like she worked there, but somehow she knew my name.

"Yes . . . yes, that's me," I stammered as I pulled my gaze away from the old man sleeping.

"Excellent, I'm Dr. Winters, your psychologist." She outstretched her hand to shake mine. I was dumbstruck. She looked different from the other doctor, and she talked with warmth. She seemed normal—or maybe better than expected. I still had a feeling in my stomach warning me of her.

"Ed?" my aunt prompted me. She never called me Ed—only my uncle. Why did she do that?

"Great to meet you." I reciprocated her handshake and smiled slightly.

"I'm Emma, Edward's aunt."

"Oh! It's great to meet you; I will certainly keep in touch," Dr. Winters responded. "Let me know if I can help you with anything." She seemed genuine. "Well, shall we begin?"

"I guess so." I was still not convinced that this new person was any different. Perhaps a wolf in sheep's clothing. I stayed on the defensive.

"All right, I see Dr. Nialliv already talked to you about confidentiality. Would you like your aunt to stay with you?" I was expecting this question. I had been giving it some thought before today.

"Nah, I think I'd like to be alone," I responded.

"We can do that. Does that sound ok to you, Emma?"

"It sure does; I'll just be around here reading my book when you are done."

Dr. Winters pointed. "Would you like to be outside or inside?"

*What an odd question.* Did I actually have an option? I didn't want to go to the prison section like last time. I didn't want to be in the hospital at all.

"I'm allowed to choose?" I replied in shock.

"Of course, this entire thing is about you." Dr. Winters smiled.

"I guess outside, if that's ok. I saw a large tree behind the hospital. Can we sit there?"

"Absolutely," she responded, grabbing two crutches nearby and moving toward the door, elevating her cast as she swung frontward and backward.

I panicked at this sight and rushed my words. "I forgot you have a broken ankle; let's stay in here."

"Come on," she yelled over her shoulder as the automatic doors closed behind her. She was quicker than she looked.

Dr. Winters laboured until we reached the foot of the oak tree. She leaned her crutches against the oak and sat down in the shade with a sigh. The branches were so old and large that they'd started to seep downward, back into the ground. Almost like the leaves were becoming new roots.

"I didn't know we could be out here," I said unprompted.

She smiled at me. "I bet everyone has more options than they realize." She paused and took a deep breath. "I checked Dr. Nialliv's notes. Although I think the assessments could be helpful, I think I'm missing your story."

I gulped and looked downward; I didn't want to tell my story. Assessments were comfortable. I didn't even know how to place my story together. I plucked grass from the ground as I talked and summarized.

"Dad died, Mom absolutely lost it, and my sister got a job elsewhere."

"And you?" she questioned.

"And I'm here," I spat with anger, defiance, and bitterness. At this moment, I truly felt cheated of my life.

"I see; what do you want?" Dr. Winters asked with kindness.

"Shouldn't you be writing this stuff down? To make notes or something?" I asked defensively. I wasn't in the mood to be probed and prodded, even though I knew this was precisely what I needed.

"My notes will come; I'm here right now. I'm not looking at my notes because I'm looking at you." And indeed, she was. I became horribly self-aware of my presence and wanted to sink into my shell. I wanted to merge into the oak tree and sit a hundred years undisturbed.

"What do I want? What do I want! What do I want . . ."

My chin began to quiver, and my voice cracked. "I want my dad. He should not be dead. I want my sister to come back home and stop doing drugs. I want her to dump her loser boyfriends. I want my mother to be a mom. I want to stop trying to put her back together; I need time. I want to kill something inside because I'm frustrated. I'm so tired."

Now my head was down in my arms and knees. I heaved, crying. Minutes went by, and I couldn't stop. Dr. Winters just sat there and waited to speak.

"I'm so sorry you lost your dad. That must have really felt like you lost a part of your life and childhood."

I began crying uncontrollably again.

"I'm so sorry you had to be a parent to your mother and sister."

I thought I couldn't cry anymore.

"I'm sorry you're hurt."

I could cry. I hadn't wept for the past year, but now I was letting it all go. So what if Dr. Winters saw? I didn't care anymore. As I regained control, I used my shirt to wipe my eyes and felt something light on my shoe. She touched it, and I looked at my shoe. On top of it was a newly plucked yellow dandelion flower. I gave a slight smile and looked at her.

"Thank you for sharing your pain. Honestly, it's an honour to experience that emotion with you. I'm proud of you."

Those were the words I was starved for. I felt emotionally exhausted. It was better than bitterness.

Over the remainder of the session, Dr. Winters listened and encouraged. She actually listened. I asked her what she thought, and she answered. Not the type of answer that an adult gives a child. The kind of answer that an adult gives to an adult. I was officially invited to participate in growing up. I thought of Adam; he always seemed to have a quality of maturity. I wondered if he was invited to adulthood. How had he managed to grow up, but I hadn't? After all, I had been caring for my mom—I should have matured faster. Didn't I deserve it? What did I deserve? Perhaps I didn't deserve to be a directionless, panic-stricken child for the rest of my life. Maybe other people didn't deserve this from me either.

# Chapter 11

A scorching, dry wind blew through my hair. I stood outside of Cherry Lake's church and looked around. Today was a Saturday, and I was volunteering to fix my emu problem. I planned to work a couple hours at the church and a couple at the clinic. I figured that it would be best to get everything over with. I could feel the heat of the sun warming my cheekbones; it was going to be a sweltering day. The church was, as I remembered, a pointed pyramid shape, only with more sides. I had a strange feeling lurking in my stomach as if something terrible was about to happen. I was nervous about doing volunteer work alone; however, I didn't think that was it.

I didn't know what to do. Was I supposed to wait outside? Should I go in? Churches were only open on Sunday mornings, right? I stood there awkwardly for a couple minutes. I was told to meet with the church pastor, who had some work for me. Walking up to the front doors, I noticed a ladder on the left side of the entrance. It was perhaps the tallest ladder I had seen in my life. It went onto the roof and beyond. It was unnecessary for the height of the rooftop. There were two doors, painted in a cracked black finish. Each door held a brass sign: a dove spiralling a ribbon around a crucifix on the left. The other door had some writing. Leaning forward, I looked at what it said.

Thou presence a mist of glory
Thy voice echoes like a lark of love
Trees bend upon Thy will
Yet the sparrows are safe

Enraptured by leagues of fire
Rebirth approaches us all

I didn't quite get it, and I'm not sure I would like it even if I understood. My family didn't attend church often, especially after Dad died, because Mom lost her license. I pulled the heavy door toward me.

*Creeeeeaak.*

*Thud.*

As I entered, a blast of air-conditioned wind brushed past me, and the door fell behind and stayed shut. I was somewhat surprised that I could just walk in. I could see a receptionist's desk with two stairs up behind the office nook. No one was there. A note written on lined paper was taped to the front of the desk. It stated:

> *Dropping off food hampers – will return before 2.*
> *Please see the pastor in the worship area if you*
> *are a guest. Be Good.*
>
> *—Alicia*

I looked around for a sign and found it. Above *bathrooms, music room,* and *kitchen* was a sign labelled *worship area* with an arrow pointing in the same direction as the music room. I ruffled my papers in my fingertips and walked down the short hallway. Before the worship area, I could hear light notes drifting effortlessly and beautifully through the air. I noticed that they were coming from the music room. Light through a frosted window indicated that this room was occupied. A single piano player sat at a black piano playing a church song I had heard before. Of course, I didn't know the name, notes, rhythm, or lyrics, but it caused me to remember sitting at church over easter. It was a pleasant melody, and the musician swayed back and forth, her golden hair swaying in the movement of the song. I wish I could have stood there longer.

Walking into the worship area, I saw rows of pews arranged in a crescent moon shape around the stage. The form of the building accommodated a large and unusual sitting arrangement. A man in grey pants and a beige collared shirt sat scowling on the circular stage at the back of the room. He appeared like a vulture: balding, hunched, and perched on his stool. He was staring at a black music stand with a pen in his mouth and wore his scowl like a tiger wears her stripes: with pride and natural ease. I guess he was the person I needed to see about working off my debt.

The pastor flipped through his papers furiously and marked them with a pen. He stopped when he saw me standing at the front of the room. As he looked up, his scowl switched to a smile. I could still hear some piano notes penetrating the wall, which somewhat comforted me. He levelled his papers, brushed his hair, and walked up to me. He seemed to walk with a type of jaunt, as if the walk was a performance. As if the aisle of the church were a fashion runway. Reaching out a hand, he said, "Hey there, young man, I'm Pastor Tom. Do you happen to be Edward?"

"Yes, sir." I handed him my volunteer papers to look over and sign.

"And with manners! How wonderful. Here, let me look at these." His frown returned. He violently flipped the paper over and cleared his throat. Twice.

"All righty then, I guess I have some work for you. But before you start, I want to ask you a couple of questions. Does that sound good to you?" He tilted his head downward and looked me directly in the eyes, alternating between left and right.

I didn't feel like I had much choice based on the tone.

"Yes, sir. Just remember to sign the forms to count these hours," I restated.

"Yes," he said with a short and pointed tone. "You will get your signature at the end. Are there two forms or just the one?"

"Just the one."

"And I sign here? Ok, that works . . . Do you go by Edward or Ed?"

"Everyone but my uncle calls me Edward."

"Well, Edward, I'm glad you could come today and help. Our janitor left us, and we have some work around here that needs to get done." He looked around and whispered, "He wasn't any good at his duties anyways. Getting him to do anything was impossible. Getting anyone to do anything around here is impossible. I heard you moved in with Matt and Emma. Have you gone to a church before?"

"Not often. Almost never," I muttered.

"Oh no? That's unfortunate; you would find this quite the community if you came here." He whispered over the back of his hand, "Preferably attending the 9 a.m. service." He chuckled. I could tell he wasn't a fan of the other congregations using the church.

"So, Edward, what do you know about the Bible?" Pastor Tom leaned onto the back of a pew and pulled out a King James Bible. It was a dark royal blue with flashy gold letters.

"Uh. Jesus? And he died? And he wanted us to care about other people while taking care of ourselves?"

Pastor Tom didn't look amused. "I guess that's a start for someone who hasn't gone to church. If you only knew what I knew . . ."

"What do you know?" I swiftly probed.

"The Pentateuch, the difference between salvation and sanctification, discrepancies between synoptic gospels, the origin of Q, and the parallels between the Abrahamic blood covenant and Christ's story." He actually smiled this time, looking proud. "You wouldn't believe how hard it is to care for these people when they don't understand as I do." He gestured to the empty pews. "Here, start by putting these into the back of the pews and moving the Bibles to their spots." He handed me a series of small yellow donation envelopes. "After that, you can clean the bathrooms and dishes in the kitchen. You would have walked by the kitchen on the way to this room."

Feeling uncertain and spiritually stupid, I took the envelope and did what he asked. Three envelopes on the back of each pew. While I moved about the worship center, Pastor Tom sat at his stool, sounding out the words of his sermon. Most of the phrases and sentences weren't understandable, at least to me. I moved a Bible from here to there and back again. Once, I opened the Bible and looked up at the pastor; he wasn't looking and wasn't going to. He was enthralled by his typing mistakes and moved his pen across the page with a mad fervour. I flipped through the pages and landed on big bold words: Mark.

*The beginning of the gospel of Jesus Christ, the Son of God;*

*As it is written in the prophets, Behold, I send my messenger before thy face, which shall prepare thy way before thee.*

For some reason, this reminded me of the Automaton. Where is he? What is he doing? Where did he go? Isn't he supposed to be a more significant part of my story?

I set the book back into the wooden slot attached to the pew. Was I missing something that I should have?

Over the next few hours, I cleaned the washrooms, kitchen, and whatever else I could find. Parts of the church were impeccably clean, while others were in much need of attention. Good thing I was here before Sunday, or the mess would not have been cleaned up. I approached the pastor, who was still reading his sermon to the ghost audience.

"Pastor Tom?"

"Yes?" He raised his reading glasses and peered at me.

"I think I've done everything you asked me."

"Ok, sounds good. I have one last task for you, and you'll be good to go."

"I have a question."

"Oh?" This seemed to grasp his attention away from his work. I suspected so. He seemed to be the person that wanted to prove that he had all the correct answers.

"I've met someone. He is a type of mentor and quite unusual." I hinted to the Automaton but said nothing as I didn't know what the pastor would have thought of my encounter. He would probably want to baptize me or something. "This unusual mentor has helped me ask questions and seems to have popped out of nowhere. He said something that has got me thinking. What is the ultimate sacrifice a person can make?"

I was reasonably confident in my question; I asked it with pride and mental organization. After all, I had been planning to ask the pastor this question for quite some time.

He looked at me and said something I wouldn't forget: "You're going to need to ask him that," and he pointed a finger upward to the roof.

"God?" I asked with a confused look.

"Huh? No!" The pastor chuckled.

"The next person that supervises your work; Alicia is back, and now I get to go home. If you want to discuss your question, you must catch me while I'm working. I'm off the clock, so go outside and talk to the roofer about how you can help. If there's nothing that he asks for, just go home." He pushed my forms back into my hand. I glanced down at the small box, which was signed with Pastor Tom's initials. My soul drooped. How can someone so invested in questions just pack up and leave? Can he at least tell me what I'm looking for? Doesn't he have any interest in helping someone at his church? I marched out, frustrated. The piano in the music room was silent, and the church secretary didn't say anything as I left. I folded the paper in half twice and shoved it into my pocket. I then looked to the side, saw the ladder, and heard footsteps on the roof.

*Thud . . . Thud . . . Thuuuump.*

Before I had stepped into the church that morning, the summer sun was hot and dry. Now it was nearly unbearable. The reddish-brown shingles were curling in the heat waves. Grasping each side of the ladder, I moved onto the roof.

What is the ultimate sacrifice a person can make? That question still burned like an ember in my mind. I couldn't give it up. What is the reason it's so important?

*Because it prescribes truth and truth prescribes meaning and meaning prescribes existence.* My inner soul echoed back the answer.

I paused midway up the ladder. What did I just hear? It was a eureka: a thought that was not mine yet came from within me. Before I could forget, I repeated it to myself.

Reason prescribes truth.
Truth prescribes meaning.
Meaning prescribes existence.

A voice broke me out of my absent-minded stare.

"Hey, how's it going? Do you need help?" I looked up to see an unshaved white-haired man in his twenties looking down at me with a smile. His skin was pale, and his eyes looked strange.

I realized that I was still standing on the ladder and continued upward.

"Oh, I'm Edward, and I'm volunteering for the church,

and I was asked to see if you needed some help. I have a couple hours before my aunt and uncle pick me up."

"Well, in that case, I could actually use a hand. I'm Sid." Sid patted a spot in the shade beside him.

"Sid?" I clarified.

"Yup. Sid." He spoke with a slight smirk.

"Good to meet you, Sid. Are you here by yourself?"

"Yeah. Today I'm getting everything set up for Monday; we are redoing the roof this week. A bit of prep work happens before everyone else shows up."

He sat down beside me with an orange tub of lotion. Flipping the cap, he squeezed out a white cream and began to rub it over his arms and neck. It was lathered on thick, not even rubbed into the skin. It reminded me of a hippopotamus caked in mud.

"I buy this stuff by the truckload. As you probably see, I'm albino, which means I get sunburned easily."

I tried not to stare, but I was fascinated. I had never met someone who was an albino before. "I guess you picked the right job then," I joked and pointed a finger toward the sun.

Sid snorted and chuckled. "Yeah, I guess you're right. Beggars can't be choosers, I guess."

He wrapped up his lathering and explained, "I just took the first job I got out of high school, and it seems to work. One day, I will have my own business. I just bought a house, so I'm looking to keep things slow for a while."

I popped out a cigarette and started to smoke. Sid seemed cool.

He sniffed and looked up. "Get that trash away from me, man." Half serious, half jokingly.

"Sorry, it's a bad habit." I took a long drag and then put it out on the eaves trough, just like my first night at my aunt and uncle's.

"It's poison. So the only part I need help with today is getting the shingles up to the roof; we will stack them up here so that everything goes quicker on Monday. They are the worst to lift, so take your time and don't worry about rushing. I won't keep you long."

For the next while, I lifted the new shingles from the backside of the church to wherever the ladder was placed. From there, Sid took the shingles and carried them up the ladder to the roof. After about two hours, we stopped, and he bought me water and some fruit from a fruit stand near the church. A deep ache lay throughout my entire back and arms. I was sore within my bones, and I continuously coughed. I had never felt like this before.

"See, I said it's poison." Sid made a smoking movement with his fingers and lips.

"I never worked this hard before," I said, still breathless as I tried to eat my nectarine.

Sid carried the conversation while I ate. "I guess there's always a first for everything. Hey, I appreciate you helping me out. There's no way I could have done this all by myself. I'm a little strapped for cash now, but here's some pay." He took out his wallet and handed me a fifty-dollar bill. I looked at the queen's face and rubbed the wrinkles out of the paper.

After a pause, I gathered my words. "I can't accept this; I'm supposed to be a volunteer. I got myself into some trouble, and I'm here to fix things."

"I don't care why you're here; I've seen you work hard. Keep it." Sid gave a smirk. "What happened?"

I told him everything; I was good at describing what had happened as I had told the story several times. Sid didn't say anything at the end but just smiled.

"You're in grade twelve?" Sid asked as he ate a slice of watermelon.

"Yup."

"Do you know Bill?"

"Yup."

"He's my brother."

"Ok, cool." I didn't know what to say and an awkward silence fell between us. I thought about what Pastor Tom had said in the church.

"Hey Sid, what's the ultimate sacrifice someone could make?"

*Sblarfff.* Sid shot water out of his nose, laughing uncontrollably.

"What's so funny? Why did you do that?"

"First of all, I didn't plan on that." Sid waved his hand at the ground. "Secondly, what type of person thinks of a question like that?"

I thought back to my epiphany. "Reason prescribes truth;

truth prescribes meaning; meaning prescribes existence."

Sid began to get a hold of himself. "Eh? Maybe? I suppose so? Does it matter to find out the answer?"

I had spent so much time thinking about how to position the question that I was uncertain if the question or the answer would be of any use. I didn't have much time to think about those other aspects before Sid came up with a solution.

"I don't think that I'm qualified to talk about that sort of thing. I'm pretty young, and I barely completed school. I know how to roof, flyfish, and hunt. Hey, I don't even know how to cook. I'm sorta the least prepared person to ask. But this is what I think: I guess anyone can die to sacrifice themselves for someone else, but I guess the ultimate sacrifice wouldn't be in death, but living for someone else. Many people give up a part of themselves daily to care for someone."

I thought of Mr. Tofs, Uncle Matt, Aunt Emma, and Dr. Winters.

"Perhaps the ultimate sacrifice is something worth doing over and over. Something worth waking up for, someone worth caring for." He ended his answer by questioning his own thoughts. "Eh? Maybe? I suppose so?"

# Chapter 12

Throughout the next week, I thought of Sid's words. I also thought of his qualifications to speak them. Although a roofer, he was more helpful than a pastor. During school, I found science and math were still confusing. In our resourcefulness class, I learned how to create a fire with two sticks and my shoelace.

The days passed quite slowly. I had a quick start to the year—I was back in school, had been to counselling twice, and had worked at the church. Even on Thursday, my back and arm muscles were sore from roofing, although not as bad as Monday when I could hardly move them. I had not started working at my uncle's shop because he was too busy managing the new hires and was seldom around the farm. I gained more chores with each passing week. Adam came by on Friday to check on me. I didn't have much to say since we typically saw each other at lunch. Jason didn't talk to me or even look at me. He seemed to have made a couple of friends with others in the class but didn't trust anyone.

On Saturday morning, I drank a steaming hot cup of coffee and sat on a baby blue rocking chair situated on the porch. The farm had seemed so sad when I first arrived, but now, I was starting to get used to the clutter and garbage. I almost didn't notice the animal sounds as they began their morning racket. I wore a ridiculous lime green poncho, shorts, and a t-shirt. I looked horrifically matched, but I didn't care. No one ever came out to the farm. I realized the people cared less about their looks here, and I was starting to feel the same way. As I gazed at a windchime, a noise broke me out of my absent-minded gaze.

"*Psst.*"

At first, I gave no reaction.

"*Psst.*"

There it was again. I stopped rocking and rose to my feet in curiosity, squinting in all directions. It wasn't the pig sleeping at the bottom of the stairs. Besides its twitching tail, the pig didn't move. My friend, the black cat, immediately scampered to the corner of the house to look around the other side of the deck. He raised his fur and bobbed his head back and forth to see where the sound had come from.

"*Psst.*" The sound arrived a third time. I saw a bronze hand beckoning me in the bushes by the forest's edge. The hand gestured out of a large conifer, making it impossible to see the rest of the person. The cat arched its back, spat, and froze, but I guessed who it was, and I was correct.

"Take a seat in my office," the Automaton gestured.

We stood in a forest opening behind the house. This land was on a downward hill, and I could still see the farmhouse's roof from this opening. There was knee-high grass that moved in waves with the breeze. Several paces away, the windmill laboured with creaks and groans. It still looked like a wizard's spire with a turning flower on top. The turning reminded me of Bartholomew, Leah's blood dialysis machine.

I looked at the Automaton closely; this was the first time I could fully see him in the sunlight. He wore coveralls, a large trapper hat, and a sticker on his chest. His torso spun around and around. Gears ticked and tocked while a large pendulum swung in the middle of his chest. The clockwork man seemed ever more real than before—not just an illusion. The sticker read: *Hello, my name is Mr. Chorales.* He sat upon a tree stump and looked at a wooden duck in his hands.

Looking up from the duck, he spoke with a slight panic. "Kid, you would never guess where I was and who I met."

I didn't know how to begin the conversation based on his odd look, dress, and duck.

"So you're real?"

"Haven't you been paying attention, kiddo? I have been real since the start. You know what? I'll let you ask me one question, and then we got to move on. I need to tell you something."

I took a seat on an adjacent stump. "Well . . ."

"Well?" the Automaton repeated with an annoyed and metallic tone.

"Never mind." I decided not to ask anything after all.

Mr. Chorales wiped his gold nose with his wrist. "Ok, here's why I'm here. Today is going to be rough. I mean really rough. But take what you learned from Sid and Pastor Tom and keep that in mind."

"What's going to happen?"

"It's not so much about worrying what will happen, but worrying about what won't happen. Do you remember what you need to remember?"

I recited it for the third time: "Reason prescribes existence, and the ultimate sacrifice is living for someone else."

"Good—the more you follow that, the more you'll understand what I'm saying. Now go on. You're about to miss your big moment."

At that instant, Uncle Matt started his truck, rolled down the window, and hollered, "EDDDDDDDDDDDDD." Birds flew out of fright away from the noise. A couple cats looked out from their homes amongst the garbage to see what made the commotion.

"Go on." The Automaton shooed me by beckoning his head. "I'll stay here; I'll be around when you get back. Remember . . ."

I looked around, half expecting the Automaton to have disappeared like the first two times I'd seen him. He sat still, looking at me with his duck in hand. I quickly turned back to the truck and walked out of the forested area.

"What were you doing in there?" My uncle beckoned to the place where I'd exited the woods. "You know you must be at the hospital soon for volunteer duty."

"Just exploring and thinking," I said truthfully.

"You have a tough time goin' into that place, eh?" My uncle started up the truck and began to head down the steep road, passing the missing signposts and Adam's family's farm.

"Yeah, I don't know why—I just do."

"Hey, don't need to give me any reason; we all got our things."

I let a couple of moments pass before asking him a question I had wondered about. "What's your thing?"

My uncle took two deep breaths before speaking. "When I was about three, I drank some medicine my mother brought home from the doctor's. I got so sick that they had to take me in. I suppose whatever I drank was a lot of calories because I'm still burning it off." He chuckled and patted his bulging belly. "My parents told me I would try eating good food, but I couldn't handle it; the medicine messed up my guts for the longest time. That's one thing. There's a lot more, but that's what I got for today."

I felt some type of peace with that story, as if I was comforted that my uncle would let me know more about him. We turned off the highway toward town. Anger and sadness started to bubble up in my soul; however, I didn't know why.

"What was Mom like growing up?"

"Your mom? A brat. I guess that is what all brothers would say. She was always caring and sensitive, she seemed to think about everyone first and herself last. I think that's a personality thingy because she has always been that way. One summer, I remember crossing the stream at the farm, and she fell in. At that time, we were both great swimmers. I was more of a floater if you know what I mean, but that got the job done. She got completely soaked, and your grandma yelled at her for that. There wasn't anything wrong, your grandma was just in one of her moods. Her anger could make Medusa turn to stone. Sometimes, it was best to leave the house and camp in the woods."

"She was mean?"

He gave a short burst of laughter with a hint of resentment. "Yeah, she was mean."

I didn't have any more questions about Uncle Matt's past; he just shared his work on the ski hill. After a break, he concluded with his update: "Sorry I have not been able to get you hours; this is just a lot more work than I realized. I'm not used to a team this big."

"No problem," I responded. And I meant it.

As we pulled up to the hospital entrance, I recognized the oak tree behind it. That was good; I thought to myself of my first meeting with Dr. Winters.

"Oh, here." My uncle wrestled around and pulled a twice-folded paper out of the truck door. I opened it up to see Pastor Tom's signature.

"One more to go." I pointed to the empty slot beside the word *Cherry Lake Regional Hospital.*

"Do you want me to come in with you?" my uncle asked.

"Nah, I'll be fine." This was the first time I was entering the hospital alone. I was still shaking and nervously fighting to get my poncho off before going in.

"All right. Just phone me when you're done. I'll just be at the shop looking over plans for the week." My uncle didn't sound convinced that I would be all right, but he didn't say anything more and just drove off.

I took my first steps into the hospital and headed toward the reception desk.

"Edward?" a nurse asked.

"Yes, that's me."

"Can I see your form?"

"Yup."

"Great, follow me this way."

Once more, we were following lines through the hospital. This time it was a dark brown line, like brown sugar. This corner of the hospital seemed calm and peaceful. There was no shouting, no blinking machines, and it seemed more like a hotel than a hospital.

"Welcome to the palliative care wing. Do you know what that means?"

"People here are old?"

"Ha! Many people are, but no. People here are dying, some faster, some sooner, but they are all in a late stage of illness.

Our job is to make them as comfortable as possible, which will be what you are doing today. Are you ok? This is not normal for most people."

"I think so." I was not lying, but I did not know how to tell the truth. I paid attention to what I was feeling in my body. I felt numb, but I felt ok, maybe a bit dizzy. The silence of the area helped. The smell was like old cinnamon: spice that'd been left out too long and lost its edge.

"Just follow the line back up to the front, and we will take care of you when you need a break. I'm so glad you're here; you will make someone's day better."

"How do I start?"

The nurse beckoned me to follow. "First, just walk the hallway. Here, I'll do it with you. Look into that room, look at that person sleeping. See—these are just people. Many of them are lonely, and some of them are bored."

*Tap. Tap. Tap.*

Our footsteps echoed down the hall. Sunlight peered through the rooms and occasionally illuminated tiny bright diamonds on the opposing hallway walls.

"They just want to be cared for and be loved. Some people here aren't going to die anytime soon, but they are sick and have trouble taking care of themselves."

The next room we walked by had an old man. *The* old man. He sat in his brown suit at the edge of the bed with a teddy bear beside him. There were freshly cut daisies on his bedside table. He was making circles with his feet, smiling and daydreaming.

"Why don't you go there and talk to that man?"

"Him?" I asked with a nervous tone. "Isn't he a little . . ." I pointed my finger and made a *crazy* swirling motion with it.

The nurse responded with a calm and collected voice. "Yes, he is crazy, but so are you and me. When people are here, they react to an abnormal situation; therefore, their unusual actions are quite normal. I can stand by the door and stay here the whole time. I know this man quite well, and he has some trouble with his memory."

"All right, I guess I need to help out sometime." I walked into the room, following the nurse and smiling at the old man. He looked at me with sudden worry and ran his fingers through his white hair. He looked like he was about to go into a panicked state. Then his eyes snapped back to the present, and he looked at both of us.

"Hello, Mr. P. Would you mind if we come and visit with you for a couple minutes today? My name is Tina; this is Edward."

"Not at all . . . pull up a seat." He gestured to two black chairs in his room. "Who are you again?"

"I'm Tina, and this is Edward."

"Are you my family? I don't really remember who they are anymore . . ."

I could understand the situation a bit better now. I saw it in his eyes—something was taken from him, and he was trying to make sense of the world.

"Can Edward read you a book?" Tina pointed to me.

"Of course! I love books. Nothing too long though, because I'm getting tired and need to get ready for 3 p.m."

"What's at three?" I asked abruptly.

"My wedding, we are getting married today at the church. I can't wait to see how beautiful my bride will be. I have been waiting for years for this moment. Did you know that I met her when I was five? She moved across the street, and I showed her around the town on the first day. When we got home, her mom gave us ice cream, and we watched bugs in the backyard. I'm the luckiest man alive. I'll be turning twenty-one soon after my wedding."

During this talk, Tina left the room. I was so fascinated with the story that I hardly noticed that she was gone. This old man thinks he is about to get married but is confused. I wonder about his wife. Is she still alive—where is she? Do they have kids and grandchildren?

Tina popped back into the room carrying three books. "These are a little older and quite short, but they are fun stories. Take a look, Mr. P., and Edward will read one to you." She laid the three books beside him on the bed and stepped back.

"Hmm." He flipped through the books. There was a fairy tale book, a book about the ocean, and a third book. While flipping through the third book, his eyes lit up. "I remember that bear! The one with the boy! I pretended to be him when I was little." He eagerly handed the book to me and handed the other two back.

I looked over the cover. *Winnie-the-Pooh* by A.A. Milne.

I cracked the book open and read aloud, pausing on every page to turn the book around and show Mr. P. the illustrations. His eyes widened, and he remembered. Halfway through the book, he stopped me.

"All this talk about adventures, and I remembered something. I was born shortly after the Great War. Things were different growing up then. We were some of the first families in Cherry Lake. At that time, it didn't really have a name. I remember reading this book in the forest with my friend from grade school. We stole it from the library. When my mother found out, she took a yardstick and slapped my knuckles until they bled. Then I returned the book with an apology note, and the librarian tried to give it to me. I don't know why, but I couldn't keep it. Maybe I was afraid of my mom. So the librarian gave me my own library card, even though I wasn't old enough to have one."

I looked at him, surprised that he could remember all these details. His eyes stopped daydreaming, and he looked back at me.

"I'm sorry—who are you? Were you saying something?"

"I'm Edward, sir, and we are reading a book."

"Ah, go on then."

I finished the book and didn't know what to say. I just closed it and smiled at Mr. P. He started to get ready for his wedding, and Tina led me out of the door and to the next one.

"He's a good man, he—"

"Leah?" I blurted out as my heart jumped up to my throat.

# Chapter 13

We passed onto the next room, and I saw a little girl lying in her bed. She was thin and had yellowish skin. She was still hooked up to tubes—different tubes, but still tubes. It still made me sick, but it didn't stop me from walking in. I forgot about the nurse. Leah wore a blue baseball cap, oversized hockey jersey, and jeans. It looked like she was on her way to a game.

"Hey, you're Edward, right?" she spoke softly and painfully.

"Yeah, I'm just helping out here at the hospital. What are you doing here? They moved you."

"Yup, they sure did. I'm not doing too good these days, but I can feel it."

"Feel what?" I asked with shock.

"I'll be out of here soon," she said softly.

I just dismissed what she said. "Can I help you? Can I sit

here?" I beckoned to a visitor's chair.

"Yeah, of course." She smiled.

"How are you doing?" I asked earnestly.

"Crummy," she said with her eyebrows lifted. "I'm just exhausted and tired of fighting."

"How can I help?"

"Can you hold my hand and tell me a story?" she requested, avoiding my eyes.

I felt deeply disturbed by this request. If I were to hold her hand, I would be touching her skin, and she looked so sickly. Not to mention I wasn't a touchy person—hugs or handshakes always made me uncomfortable. I also panicked at the second request. A story. I didn't have a story—at least not yet. Old people have stories. People who go on adventures have stories. My own story was as enjoyable as roadkill on the side of the road.

Wham—and it's over.

End of the story, the lights fade out.

Leah was still looking at me. Something welled up inside me, and I looked her in the eyes. I was controlled and compelled by a virtuous feeling. I dragged my visitor's seat over to the side of the bed. Looking back into the hallway, I could see that Tina had left and I was alone. I sat down beside Leah and took her hand. She was freezing, and she pulled a blanket over her waist. I remembered the piano notes floating through the church; they seemed to return as a memory of courage sailing in the breeze.

"I don't really have many stories—what if I made one up?"

Leah nodded. She reminded me of what my sister could have been.

"Ok, here it goes, the story of the rabbit and the golden pocket watch. Once upon a time, there was a very fluffy rabbit named Troy. Troy wasn't an ordinary rabbit; he spoke, cooked, read the newspaper, and could do just about anything you or I can do. One day, Troy was sipping his coffee in his rabbit hole when he heard a strange sound. *Click. Click. Click.* Looking out of his hole, he saw something on the ground in the woods. Even though Troy was a clever rabbit, he had never seen a pocketwatch and didn't know what it was. Looking off into the distance, he watched a hunter walk away. Troy has seen lots of hunters before, and he saw some of his friends disappear. So, like always, Troy snuck back into his rabbit hole, turned off the lights, and stayed very quiet. *Click. Click. Click.* The shiny circle still made noise even after the hunter left. *Click. Click. Click.* Troy went out and looked at the weird shiny thing. He opened it up and saw two lines moving around with gears, springs, and hinges. 'What is this? What do I do with this new thing?' Puzzled, he brought it into his house but still didn't know what to do with it. 'This thing is so shiny and round.' Troy tried to think about what else was shiny and round. Leaves? No. Eyes? No—that can't be it.

"Troy had his feet up by a campfire and sang with his friends one night. Through the tree canopy and clouds, Troy could see something. A large object he had seen every night. The Moon. 'Ah!' he thought. 'That must be what it is. The thing the hunter dropped is a star! It moves in cycles—day and night, round and glimmering brightly. A star in my pocket! I must be the luckiest rabbit in the world. Who am I to have this thing? What should I do with it?'"

I looked down at Leah; she was lying there with her eyes closed. She looked so peaceful. I didn't know if she was asleep, so I left the chair where it was, and I got up. I pulled my hand away from hers and began sneaking into the doorway. There was a clock in the hallway beside the door. *Click. Click. Click.*

*

I remember it was the following Tuesday. I was cleaning the chicken coop when I looked up and saw my uncle approaching. He looked down at his cowboy boots while he walked and shuffled more than usual. He seemed worried. Really worried. What was he going to say? A turkey chased his boots and waddled back and forth, trying to track the motion of each foot. Both of them ended up at me.

"Um, Edward . . . I have bad news . . . I know you went to the hospital last week and met some really good people. As you know, Leah was sick for a very long time, and last night she passed away. I'm sorry to tell you this, but I think it's important you know as soon as we do. After all, you're Adam's friend, and his whole family could use some help."

I didn't say anything for a while. I just stood there with

my jeans, ripped t-shirt, gloves, and a bucket. My boots were caked with mud and chicken poop. I sighed heavily. Another one is gone—and what's the cruel reason this time? Now, Uncle Matt is expecting me to help Adam? I have never been able to help anyone, especially with something like this. I also did not have the numb feeling that I was used to. This grief floated in the air like a giant balloon indoors. It's noticeable and inconvenient, but it's light and airy. What am I supposed to feel with death? It's different every time.

"What should I do?" I asked.

"For yourself or Adam?" My uncle wiped a tear away from the corner of his eyes and turned his head quickly around.

"Both," I responded.

"Maybe for yourself, you can talk to Dr. Winters this week, and for Adam . . . Maybe you should take him for a hike."

"A hike? I don't know many spots around here."

"Why don't you hike the Bull's Horn? One starting path is at the end of our property right there." My uncle pointed a chubby finger toward the forest's edge. "You just go a while past the edge, and you'll find a path of switchbacks. Although you might want to wait until after the funeral."

"The funeral?"

"Yeah . . . I guess it will be on Friday morning. You won't have to go to school that day."

"Thanks . . ." I looked down and pondered everything. I needed to talk to the Automaton. He knew it was going to happen. If I needed him, he would show up. Or would he?

I finished my remaining Tuesday chores and went to my bedroom to wrap up my homework. My mind was racing, and I leaned out the window to have a cigarette. My supply was dwindling by now, and I'd started to ration them. I had tried to bribe some store clerks to allow me to purchase more, but they didn't budge. They remembered me as the emu guy. I looked at the night sky's constellations, and the black cat sat on the window frame beside me. Meteors fell in the eastern horizon, popping out of view behind a cloud and disappearing behind a mountain. As I smoked, I petted the cat and wondered. How could someone be here one moment and then gone the next? This perspective was considerably more disturbing this time—I didn't think much when my dad died. I just felt. Tears welled up in my eyes, but I could not cry. I didn't know what to do with my body. I felt awkwardly assembled and put together, straddling the border between functional and lost. When will I die? Will others feel the same thing when they hear the news? What will the sunrise be like the next day? If I'm not here, where will I be? At what point will I be forgotten, even in the memories of others?

I looked at the cat. "Sheesh, I'm starting to sound like the Automaton—the cranky, rusty man."

For the rest of that week, I stayed in that state of limbo, not together but also not apart. Where was I? I tried to describe my experience to Dr. Winters; I don't think she understood, but that was ok. I didn't want to be understood. I just didn't want to be alone. I had a difficult time staying focused in school. For the entire week, Adam was away, and I didn't talk to him over the phone. On Wednesday, Bill and I exchanged glances and didn't need to say much. I wasn't looking forward to Friday, but part of me was curious. What would happen next? I never did see the Automaton; he never showed up. I remembered his last words to me. *Now go on; you're about to miss your big moment.* Was it my moment at the hospital? Did I do something good? I kept thinking how lucky the rabbit was to have a star in his pocket. I think I was beginning to understand what this story meant.

# Chapter 14

I couldn't get the lines right. I would move the iron over one side of the shirt, unintentionally making another line elsewhere. It was infuriating. I remember my father teaching me to iron; however, it was a skill so rarely used. Since the farmhouse was small, Aunt Emma always did her ironing on the porch. Steam from hot coffee and the iron leapt into the cold air, portraying a graceful dance. The wood from the porch creaked like a sailing boat as I shifted my weight back and forth.

As we arrived for the funeral, I noticed that the church looked different from before. The outside looked a little cleaner, and the grass was a darker shade of green. I wore brown pants, black dress shoes, a blue tie, and a white shirt. As I entered the church, I remarked at most of the town's arrival.

I saw Mr. P. being led by a nurse. He sat at the back of

the sanctuary and looked around, confused and wide-eyed. His umbrella was still around his arm. I bet he wondered why a funeral was happening instead of his wedding. Leah's family wasn't in the room yet; they must have met before the funeral. Aunt Emma, Uncle Matt, Sid, Bill, and their family sat in the same pew. These benches were hard and uncomfortable, but everyone seemed to manage. At the front of the room was a small casket covered with half a dozen yellow flowers. Similar flowers were tossed out by Adam's father in Leah's hospital room the day I met her. A wooden cross had been raised in the back of the church, lit up from behind. It wasn't there before, and I wondered why they would have a movable cross in a church; it seemed redundant.

Beginning the ceremony, the family walked in with a single piano playing notes of a hymn. I didn't know what the melody was—after all, we never regularly attended church—but it sounded upbeat and hopeful. Nearly the whole family was crying, but Adam was not. I wondered what was going on. I had lost a sister, but not like this.

A new pastor began the service, someone I had never met before. He talked a lot about the Bible, God, and heaven. I listened attentively, but I didn't quite understand what he said. After he finished, a carousel slide projector was brought up to the front of the church, a screen was pulled down, and lights were dimmed. I still had difficulty focusing; it reminded me of math class.

There was a photo of Adam's family; his mom was

pregnant, presumably with Leah. The following slide was a baby wrapped in a yellow knitted blanket. Another photo of Leah—this time, she was holding a fish above her head. Another image, a school photo. Another one—she was celebrating her eighth birthday. Next one: she smiled and hugged a stuffed animal in the hospital. Next one: she had stickers all over her face, and a nurse beside her had a hot pink wig. That was the last photo. As they shut off the projector, I felt my eyes give a flash, and I saw an outline of a rabbit on the projector screen! Then it was gone, just like an illusion before my eyes. Was it just me? I rubbed my eyes and focused on the screen, but I saw nothing.

Adam's father rose to his feet. "Hey, everyone, I'm Ethan, Leah's father. Thank you for coming today to celebrate Leah's life. I greatly appreciate your support over the years." His voice quivered with the last few words. He paused and then began again. "We couldn't have made it without you." He began to cry and walked back to his seat.

*

"So, how was that?" my aunt asked my uncle and me as we walked back to the truck. I had a Nanaimo bar in one hand and apple crisp in the other.

"That wasn't right," my uncle replied.

I didn't say anything, and we walked in silence.

As we got back to the truck, I asked, "Was that funeral like Dad's?"

Both Aunt Emma and Uncle Matt looked at each other. I think I caught them off guard with that question. I didn't really remember what had happened and wanted to recall the ceremony.

"I think it was different," my uncle blurted out. My aunt gave him a look that suggested he be careful with his next few words. "Leah was a kid, and your dad was a father; losing both is terrible, but I think we were wondering what would happen next. We were worried about what would happen to you for your father's funeral rather than how Adam's family would cope."

"Yeah . . . I guess we didn't cope."

Aunt Emma encouraged, "Honey, you did the best with what you had."

"All of us?" I hinted with my voice that I doubted her statement. After all, how could she say that after my sister moved and my mom left?

She raised her eyebrows and said seriously, "Yes—all of you."

I changed out of my dress clothes and walked to the stream that cut across the west side of my aunt and uncle's property. I noticed something on the side of the path. *Rattle, clank eeek, click-click.* It was the Automaton who held a stick high above his head. He was hitting something just above the ground. As I moved around the bend, I could see that he was beating a skunk cabbage in the tall grasses. His arms made metallic sounds with each swing.

"What are you doing?" I asked.

"This dumb plant," he responded.

"Why are you hitting it?"

"Oh . . . you know," he said through a swing.

I didn't know. After a couple more whacks, I regained attention to my thoughts. "Leah's funeral was today."

The Automaton gave the plant one last heavy whack, more substantial than the rest. Then he looked at me, leaned on his stick, and sighed. I didn't know he could sigh; after all, he didn't have lungs, I could see through his chest. A flywheel inside his abdomen began to speed up. He poked the ground and looked up with his copper eyes.

"How did you say goodbye?"

"I went to her funeral."

"No, before that—the same day we talked when you went to the hospital."

"I sat beside her, held her hand, and told her a story about a rabbit. I just made up the story."

"All stories are made up. If they weren't made, they would not have been stories, but that's beside the point." He reached his right hand over to his left elbow. He made something click and then rotated his left forearm ninety degrees. From there, he detached his left forearm and held it between his knees. He then used his right hand to adjust some rods inside the arm. "How did it go?"

"Sitting by her and saying a story?"

"Absolutely," the Automaton responded while he shook

his detached left arm. The arm's fingers clasped inward and outward in a violent motion.

"It was good; I guess it was good for both of us."

"Why was it good? Didn't it feel uncomfortable?"

"Yeah, but I was able to give her something she needed, and I guess it felt good to know I made a difference." I paused. "I guess I helped make her last days a little easier than if I had stayed home."

"If you're at home and comfortable, who benefits?" He momentarily stopped with his arm and looked up at me. It made me very uncomfortable.

"I guess no one," I responded. I first thought of Leah, but then thoughts surrounding my journey sprouted. I needed exposure to see, although I was uncertain what I was seeing in the first place.

The Automaton reattached his arm with a click and smiled. "You're growing up. If something is uncomfortable, it might mean you are doing something right. It might also mean that you're just being stupid. Remember to rest, but don't forget to get out there and live your life."

"Are you coming to the stream with me?" I gestured in the general direction of where I was heading.

"I suppose so." He tossed his stick across the grassy field, where it stuck in the ground like a javelin.

The Automaton and I walked for about fifteen minutes until we reached the stream. I could see minnows dancing between the middle of the creek and the shadowy overhang of the plants and land. I took off my socks and shoes and rolled up my pants slightly. I placed my feet in the icy water, allowing it to shock my system. I felt disturbed that I was so calm. I sat there beside the Automaton in silence, watching frogs hopping on the bank of the stream. Once again, I found myself sitting amongst blue lupines, my favourite kind of flower. These flowers reminded me of castles from some fictional drama. Dragonflies hovered and hunted. Giant bees danced with flowers and looked like cotton balls painted yellow with black stripes. Looking up at the sky, I saw a bald eagle hovering above the nearby field, not flapping its wings but staying in the same place. While drifting off into my imagination, I didn't realize that the Automaton had left. I was sitting there by myself, captivated by my own thoughts.

"Edward?"

I nearly jumped out of my skin. I was so focused on what was happening around me and my imagination that I'd lost myself. Turning around, I saw Adam. He had on a ragged blue shirt with shorts and sandals.

"Oh hey," he said, sitting beside me, taking off his sandals and dipping his feet into the water. He gave a sigh, and I looked down at a rock I rolled around between my fingers.

"I'm sorry about your sister."

Adam picked up a pebble and threw it into the pond.

*Splink.*

"Don't be. She had it rough, but Leah had a great life before getting sick. I kinda wonder what we are going to do now." I stayed quiet and just looked at him. "Every day, we would stop by the hospital—it's been like this for two years. Now what?"

*Splink.* Another pebble hit the water's surface, causing the minnows to flee.

He continued, "I guess we will find out. She wasn't supposed to be this sick."

"How can I help?" I asked. I didn't know if this was sincere or just a distraction to fill the silence.

Adam began to cry but quickly gathered himself. He wiped his eyes and looked up toward the sky. "Honestly, I don't know. Maybe just listen . . . or maybe you could tell me why you're here. I don't want to always avoid that topic forever."

This time I didn't hesitate. I had already talked about it with Dr. Nialliv and Dr. Winters. "My dad died a while back, and my mom lost it. I stopped going to school, and I took care of my mom. I would hide money inside a plastic bag in the flour container. She stopped baking and cooking, so I knew she would never find it. I had to stop her from spending it. I remember one time I found her standing on the railing of our apartment balcony, looking down. When I entered the room, she began crying and locked herself in the bathroom. The next thing I knew, I was in a taxi going to my aunt and uncle's farm while my mom was in a hospital. I don't think I will ever get to live with her again."

"Don't you have a sister too?" Adam asked.

"Yeah, she moved out after Dad died. She moved to a

small community outside the city, but I haven't talked to her. I think she just lost hope and became interested in her boyfriend. She never showed up for my mom and me when we needed it. How can someone leave family just like that?"

"What would you say if you saw her again?" Adam questioned.

Flashes of anger crossed my mind, followed by streaks of sadness.

"I love you, and I forgive you for leaving me," I muttered.

"Would you mean it?"

"Absolutely," I said without complete certainty.

We sat there with our feet in the icy water and sunlight warming our backs. The brook sang out its hymn of peace and comfort: ripples of water on rocks and crickets chirping. As the sun began to set, we silently lamented the cruel chapter fate had delivered and pondered what it meant.

*

That weekend, I didn't do much. Uncle Matt stayed around the farm more than usual and did most of the chores. I guess he was making up for the time he was working. On Sunday afternoon, we were again reading in the living room. This time, the black cat managed to jump through my open window upstairs, waltzed down, and sat on my chest. My uncle lifted his eyebrows at the cat and glanced over to my aunt, who shook her head and then looked back to me. He grunted, picked up his vintage car magazine, and began reading again.

After a few minutes, he placed his magazine back down. "Hey, Ed, wanna see something cool? I've just got an idea— it's a surprise."

After the funeral, I wasn't in the mood for much. I just wanted to rest and play my guitar. But this snagged my curiosity. "Sure, where are we going?"

"Like I said, a surprise." Uncle Matt had a mischievous smile on his face.

The two of us climbed into his pickup truck and began down the steep road. After driving on a couple back roads, I saw it. A massive lodge behind a large gravel parking lot. We were at the ski hill that Jason's father owned. "We're here; let's go." Uncle Matt beckoned as we got out of the truck.

"Should we be here?" I asked hesitantly.

"Absolutely. You know, quality inspection," Uncle Matt joked.

"What are you going to show me?" I asked while struggling to exit the truck's deformed passenger door.

"Keep up." Uncle Matt was already ten strides ahead of me. While he was considerably overweight, he could still move quickly if he wanted to. I got out of the truck, and we made our way to the front doors. My uncle reached into his back pocket, pulled out a key, and we were in.

"Woah," I said with amazement.

The outside was still under construction, but a large

amount of the inside was finished. The arched ceilings were at least three stories tall, and the interior was decorated like a cabin. There was a mural of constellations and northern lights on the soaring ceiling. This reminded me of those large cathedrals from Europe.

"The coolest part about that," my uncle lifted a finger to the ceiling, "is that the stars are all in the right place. The artist worked on making it as real as possible."

While staring up at the mural, I remembered my dream. The one about standing on the sinking ground and the sky disappearing to show the cosmos. Of course, the mural was beautiful; it wasn't the same look but the same idea.

We continued through the construction site, wandering past the gift shop, cafeteria, bathrooms, and rental shop. It was amazing to see how it was getting put together. I went to a ski lodge when I was younger, but it wasn't like this. It made me wonder why it was built; it wasn't because Cherry Lake could pay for this. It was like an immaculate cathedral built in the middle of the desert—it didn't make much sense unless people would travel to see it.

My uncle and I turned to one another as we heard footsteps coming down the hallway. Who would be here on a Sunday? We went to see who it was—it was Jason and his father. They were arguing about something, I couldn't tell what. When they saw my uncle and me, they stopped. Jason's father wore a pink dress shirt, black dress pants, and black dress shoes.

"Ah, Mathew! Surprised to see you here on a Sunday."

"Oh, I just wanted to show Ed around the ski hill, toss some inspiration around to the younger generation. What's happin' with yah?"

"Indeed! I've brought Jason here to help me figure out some details. You know, I want him to have a say since we have moved out here for this project."

"I say we burn it to the ground," Jason said with bitterness.

"*What?*" Jason's father slapped the back of his head, and Jason stayed silent. Jason's father gritted his teeth and gave another hit. "Anyway, feel free to stick around; I know there is lots to see." Jason's father continued on as if nothing had happened.

Despite his offer, Uncle Matt and I drove back to the farm; I felt uncomfortable around Jason. I would see him at school, and he would always avoid me. To him, I was a traitor. Distant dark clouds began to fill the horizon and threaten a storm.

We talked a bit about the ski lodge, but there was an awkward silence between my uncle and me. I wanted to say something about Jason and his father, but I didn't know how to. I still hadn't told my aunt and uncle about how Jason choked me at school that day. I figured that I could keep that between us. I guess I deserved it.

"Whose car is that?" I pointed to a dusty blue sedan parked in front of the farmhouse.

"I don't know. I've never seen that car before . . . huh."

Walking through the front door, I stopped in my tracks.

There was my aunt, smiling and drinking tea with my sister.

# Chapter 15

"Oh hey, Edward—you're looking good." Tabitha hugged me while I stood dumbstruck in the doorway. I stood there with my arms by my side—I did not raise my hands to hug her. I just stood there: a person apart from themselves as a rift in time and space, shoulders drooping. I felt like I was standing in the rain, unable to pull myself up. I expected to feel anger, a pulsing wave of energy going through my fists; however, I felt nothing but waves of sadness, powerlessness, and irrelevancy. Thunder rumbled off into the distance.

"Are you ok?" Tabitha grabbed me by the arms and tried to look me in the eyes, but I looked at the wooden floor: at the white teacup shards I could not pick up the night I arrived. A lightning flash bounced off the walls and lit up the room before fading into the corners.

"Edward?" She squeezed my arms tighter. My aunt and uncle just watched.

Before I knew it, I turned around, wrestling away from my sister. I reached for the doorknob and ran down the steps. Massive raindrops painted the yellow porch in darker hues, making the air seem heavier. The pig raised his head to the sky, closing his eyes and standing in the downpour. I began to run as fast as my feet could carry me. I had no plan of where I was going. When I passed the workshop, the rain had turned to hail and pelted my back as I ran. I noticed it but didn't care. I could see the fence at the forest's edge—the metal windmill stood by it. I wanted to get to the woods where I could be alone; even the Automaton couldn't follow me there. I brushed rain, or tears, from my cheeks as I ran and wiped my nose. The fence came closer and closer.

*Creak, creak, whirrlllll.*

The windmill was twisting violently in the wind. Lightning made each tree cast a harsh shadow on another—the forest looked like a series of jagged fangs. A blueish flash lit up the face of the mountain. It looked just like a rabbit. That stopped me in my tracks; I slowed to a walk as I neared the fence. Then a feeling in my gut welled up in my eyes. The hairs on my neck stood up, and I felt water and mud squishing between my toes. I was standing in a puddle.

*Szzzzzzzbooooooooommmm.*

Lightning struck the windmill and knocked me down. I lost consciousness and straddled the boundary of life and death. Water and air. Did I land face up or face down in the puddle? Was I finally dead? Could I finally rest? The corners of consciousness blended into a bright pillar: on top sat a speckled peacock. That was it.

# Chapter 16

I didn't know where I was; it wasn't the hospital. I was sitting on the sandy ground next to a large, circular body of water. All around me, palm trees were blowing in the desert wind. Instead of being surrounded by mountains, I was in the middle of towering dunes; one couldn't have climbed up even if one had all the strength in the world. I leaned over to look at my reflection in the water. I jumped back at what I saw: my face was the face of the Automaton. I reached up and touched my cheekbones, eyes, and lips. I didn't feel gears, widgets, or metal when I did this. I felt smooth skin, my normal human skin, full of life and youthful. I breathed a sigh of relief to think that I was still myself. I leaned forward once more to look at my face. I still wore the look of the Automaton, but it was my face. It was as if I were both the Automaton and Edward simultaneously. What did this mean? I looked up to see the sky and noticed something curious—I could see everything, but there seemed to be no source of light, no sun. Instead, everything was a light source, and the sand emitted a blinding look.

As I noticed this, I looked back into the water a third time and saw my regular face, the face of Edward. I looked down at my hands in the water. Beneath the water, they were shiny and metallic, the hands of clockwork. I waded into the pool, each step bringing me closer to the middle until I needed to tread water. Instinctively, I floated facedown into the water, blowing bubbles. These bubbles ran up my face and woke me up in doing so. It was as if I were passing through water into the air. Then from air into the sand and finally—nothing.

I could move my fingers, but that was about it. I couldn't feel my legs or feet, and my neck was secured. I was placed in a bed in a dimly lit room. Green, red, orange, and white lights flickered on a machine next to my bed. A beige curtain was all around me, hung by a rail from the ceiling. I could hear breathing next to me. My heart started racing, but I couldn't move; I was secured in place by medical equipment. What happened? "Where am I?" I whispered so that the breathing voice next to me couldn't hear. Am I alone?

I tried to recollect what had happened. I remembered the oasis in the desert and becoming the Automaton, but what happened before? For a few minutes, I worked hard to remember; however, nothing happened. Then suddenly, I felt disturbed and remembered the lightning striking the windmill and my loss of consciousness. I could almost remember the smell. I'm not dead? How? Why?

Another thought lingered in my mind, but I had difficulty bringing it forward. Something disturbing—why was I running? It took a couple of minutes before my memory flooded my consciousness like the previous thought. My sister? Was that a dream, or was she really back? Yes, she was back, but why? Why did she care right now? Didn't she know I didn't want to ever see her again? I thought that was why she left.

Another trail of thought passed through my mind. My time in the oasis was an odd observation that seemed more real than reality. Now that I was awake, the experience of the oasis appeared trivial and unremarkable. But that was curious—it was remarkable, even if it wasn't an actual experience. Can it be true? What does it mean?

My head was swimming with questions, and I lay there with my thoughts. In fact, I had so much on my mind that I tuned out the person breathing next to me. About thirty minutes passed, and the person behind the curtain started coughing uncontrollably. It started so suddenly and loudly that I jumped and felt my heart leap. Since I was in bed, I couldn't move with my reaction, and searing pain shot all over my body in the blazing heat. I whimpered and lay still while the coughing went on. It continued for about twelve minutes until I heard someone march in, pull back the curtain, and help the person next to me. Tears were welling up in the corners of my eyes. I couldn't move; I would have curled into a fetal position under the blankets if I could. It was a pretty pathetic thing for a young man, or was it?

"There you go, drink this; I'll move your pillows so you can sit up."

"T . . . t . . . thanks," said a raspy voice.

"You're welcome. Would you like something to read now that you're awake?"

"Ye . . . y . . . yes. Yes please."

"All right, I'll see what we got and bring back some options."

"I . . . I-I . . . I. Ap . . . a . . . appreciate . . . i . . . i . . . it."

"You're welcome."

The footsteps left the room, and silence filled it. The voice owner cleared his throat several times and made a humming sound.

"Hello?" I squawked across the curtain. My voice cracked as I used it first, and I chuckled under my breath.

"Hello?" the owner of a raspy voice responded. "Yo . . . y . . . you're aw . . . awake?"

"Yes, who are you?"

I saw a hand reach its fingers around the curtain and pull. The curtain slid along the top rail, getting stuck every so often.

"Bill?"

Bill lay there on his side of the room. Both sides of the room were dark; however, I could see his outline because he was closer to the window and farther from the door.

"E . . . Ed . . . Edward?" he stuttered, then immediately responded by coughing, bringing his hand to his neck, and holding it here. I followed his hand with my eyes and saw something I would never forget. The top of his neck was red and indented as if he was branded with a curved iron, but the burn never blistered. He was in a hospital gown like me and handcuffed to the bed.

"Bill!? What are you doing here?" I asked with a panic.

Bill sat back on his bed and began to sob uncontrollably. He stayed this way for a couple of minutes; even when the nurse came, he couldn't stop. She began to gently help him back down, but he refused by pushing her away.

"Leave . . . m . . . me . . . be."

She put a hand on his back, giving it a light rub, and then gave us a pitiful smile before leaving. She left a stack of books on a bedside table.

I asked again after Bill regained himself, "What happened?"

"I . . . I . . . It . . . t . . . tried to . . . to . . . ki . . . k . . . kill myself." He made a hanging gesture with his hands and punched the mattress next to him. *Thram. Thram.* Bill's fists sunk deep into the mattress. This scared me.

My eyes widened. "I'm sorry, Bill. I would have said something at the funeral."

"Me t . . . too," he responded.

Again, we sat just the two of us in the dim room. Him with his marks around his neck and me with . . . with what exactly? I didn't quite know yet.

"Y . . . y . . . you?" he asked, pointing to my legs and neck brace.

"I was running to the forest and got hit by lightning."

Bill's eyes widened. "S . . . seriously?"

"Yeah . . . I think I may have died. Or dreamed?" I questioned myself. I didn't tell him why I was running in the first place; I didn't think he needed to know. It was an overreaction. At least in hindsight, it made no sense.

"W . . . what . . . was . . . was . . . it . . . like?" Bill asked.

I chuckled a second time. I didn't understand why I laughed so much, but I guess I was grateful to be alive.

"Well, you see—it's a little foggy." I pointed to my head. "But I remember seeing a quick flash that lit up the whole mountainside, and then I saw the windmill out of the corner of my eye; it was struck. I was standing in a puddle nearby. I didn't even think. Then I remember seeing some stuff."

I looked Bill in the eyes deciding if I should tell him what I saw. "Before going out, I saw a peacock on top of a golden pillar, and the next thing I knew, I was waking up in the desert."

Bill gave a snort and then realized that I was serious.

"It was sandy, and I looked at my reflection in a pool of water, and it wasn't me. When I dove into the pool, I became something else."

"W . . . wh . . . what?"

I gave a sigh. "It's silly. I don't even know what happened. I fried my brains."

"I . . . w . . . wa . . . want . . . to. Know." Bill struggled to get the words out.

"Ok, here it goes. I became an automaton." There! I said it; I had never told anyone else about this before. "A being made of metal and clockwork parts."

"A . . . a . . . man-made . . . man?"

"I guess so. I don't know what it means." I looked over to Bill to see if he had any insight, but he shrugged his shoulders and started coughing again. I felt terrible, both because of the burns and hearing about Bill. I hoped that he could see Dr. Winters.

A doctor quickly marched into the room. He was older with a white mustache and held a clipboard. Behind him, a nurse followed his steps. "Ah, Edward, is it?" He looked over his glasses as he talked to me.

"Yes, that's me."

"Welcome to our hospital, Edward. You're a lucky man to be alive. What do you remember?"

"Umm . . . I just remember getting hit by lightning, and then everything went black. I think I died or had a dream or something."

"All right, so you do remember the lightning—good. Your aunt and uncle found you lying in a pool of water. You have some pretty severe burns, and we don't know exactly how you fell, so that is why we stabilized your head. There is a possibility of nerve damage; however, you should be able to recover well at your age. You know, you're lucky that you didn't drown."

I thought back to my dream, death, or hallucination; I don't know what that experience was. Whatever it was, it was odd; although many things were strange lately. I went into the oasis and lay front down in the water—being transformed by it rather than drowning. Maybe that was what happened in real life?

The doctor continued. "Today is Monday, and you had your accident last night; would you like me to give your family a call and invite them down to see you now that you're awake?"

I was going to immediately respond with a yes, but I didn't know how they would react. What would my sister say? A sick, twisted part of my mind thought this was revenge for her leaving. She would need to take a look at what she had done. This was her fault.

"Yes, you can tell them."

"Excellent." Both the nurse and the doctor left the room and left me there with my thoughts. Bill reached over and pulled his privacy curtain around him without saying a word.

I lay there unmoving for a while, unsure what to do. Should I say something to Bill? Perhaps he wanted some privacy from my family and me. Who knows that he's in here at the hospital? At least his parents and his brother should know, right? Every so often, a person would walk down the hallway, or Bill would start a coughing spasm again. I felt that the best thing I could do was nothing at all. So that was what I did; I lay perfectly still in the bed, feeling sore and flashes of pain radiating up from my burns. About seventeen minutes passed, and my aunt and uncle raced into my room. I fully anticipated my sister to follow them in, but the doorway was empty, and no one came.

"Where's Tabitha?" I said with a bitter tone.

My aunt sighed deeply and responded, "At the motel . . . She feels terrible for what happened, and we didn't tell her that you could have visitors."

"What were you thinking? Could you have been denser?" My uncle turned a shade of red. "You're not just gambling with your life anymore, so stop acting like you are."

One of Bill's spastic coughs caused the three of us to startle and change our gaze before looking at each other again.

"I'm sorry . . . I was so upset, and didn't like being surprised," I said.

"How do you think I felt when I pulled you out of the mud, covered in black marks?" My uncle waved his hand toward me. "A little upset? A little surprised? Smarten up. You're not a kid anymore; you're a man."

\*

That weekend's lightning strike caused two things: it formally introduced me to manhood and allowed me to see that I was becoming an automaton. I had never thought of the point of becoming a man. I thought it was when you turned eighteen, your first serious relationship, or your first time drinking. I then realized that my idea of manliness and manhood were two separate things. Men go a lifetime without being invited to be a man. What kind of identity is that? I felt that there wasn't anything left to prove. I did it: I grew up.

Now what?

# Chapter 17

Adulthood is an imposter syndrome of the highest order—faking it until making it. I had a lot of time in that hospital room. I relied on others to support me with nearly everything: going to the bathroom, moving my feet, and changing my bandages. I left the TV on almost all the time; the noise helped me as I zoned in and out to process my possible death. The whole event didn't seem real; it certainly didn't *feel* real. I was horribly repulsed when we peeled back the dressings and saw the burns covering my body. They looked hideous and caused me to look away. Topical creams, ointments, and treatments needed to be lathered around the wounds. It turned out that I didn't hurt my neck or back and was allowed to lie in bed without a neck brace.

After the first couple of days, I realized that I had become accustomed to the comings and goings of the hospital. I also felt that my brain had finally caught up with my body—no, my spirit. My panic around the hospital had been completely erased and replaced by the terror of being alone. I finally understood why I needed to sit beside Leah, hold her hand, and tell her a story while dying. What was my story? I was still trying to figure that out. What had happened, and what would happen? I pre-emptively decided to erase the expectations of my life and simply treat myself as if I were worth more than garbage. I decided that if I wasn't dead, there was probably a good reason, even if I was the person to determine it. What was the reason? I thought back to my day at the church.

Reason prescribes truth
Truth prescribes meaning
Meaning prescribes existence

I still didn't know how to handle this knowledge; my mind hadn't worked in this manner before. I wondered what Bill thought. He was moved to another place shortly after my first day in the hospital. My sister had still not come to see me. From what my aunt and uncle said, she stayed at the motel for a couple days. I wondered how she had heard that I was at my aunt and uncle's in the first place. Did Mom say anything? I didn't even know if Mom had a phone or would know my sister's number.

"Ok, today's the day." A nurse looking down at a clipboard walked into my room. The bed to my right stayed absent after the days that Bill left. "Let's see about getting you back home. How are you feeling?"

"Great, actually," I responded with pain but energetically.

"That was quite the event. I'm glad you've made a great recovery." The nurse smiled.

*

I sat there at an intersection with my uncle in his truck. He didn't say much, but I knew he was still upset with me, perhaps also upset with my mom since he was now in this position. I was bandaged up and happy to get out of the hospital. Every curve and bump in the road reminded me of my pain, causing a flare of discomfort. I kept the seatbelt loosened over my shoulder so I could lean forward to relieve the pain in my legs. At this point, I was excited to get back to the farm and maybe see my sister. This had been going on for long enough.

I had entered the hospital because of my body but healed something else. As we sat at the intersection, my mind ticked with ideas and feelings I had processed in the hospital. I dazed off in an absent-minded trance.

*Thump.*

A sound like a door being slammed came from a distance. Neither Uncle Matt nor I reacted.

*Thump.*

There it was again, a little louder.

*Thump.*

Both Uncle Matt and I began to look around—what's that sound?

*Thump.*

Something smacked the back windshield of the truck, causing both of us to jump and Uncle Matt to swear. A watery mark was left on the rear window. A wide eye appeared through the front of the windshield and was carried off through the intersection. A bald eagle clutched a massive lake trout, the trout still alive and fighting. The eagle had difficulty lifting the fish above the ground, smacking more cars with the fish. Far down the road, the eagle dropped the fish into bushes and took off in the opposite direction.

"Did we just see that?" I broke the silence.

"Yeah. I've never seen that before," Uncle Matt said, awestruck.

"An omen?" I asked in a joking manner.

My uncle laughed. "What do you think it means?"

"Don't be the fish. Or maybe be the fish, but don't be the eagle . . . Maybe the fish is better because he got away."

"What sense are you talking about? You're the one who ran out during a lightning storm," my uncle said with frustration and amusement.

"I think it knocked some sense into me."

"Good, it better have. Don't do that again."

"Yup," I said. At this, my uncle seemed shocked but didn't say anything. "I will call Tabitha when we get home and straighten some things out."

Uncle Matt lifted his eyebrows. "Yeah?"

"Yeah."

And that was what I did. As soon as I stumbled over the top steps of the porch and into the kitchen, I picked up the shiny red rotary phone that hung on the wall.

"Hello? Yes—can you send me to room 27? Thanks."

A faint female voice answered. "Hello? This is Tabitha."

I stood there in silence for a moment, wrapping the phone's cord around and around my finger. I was tempted to hang up. To run away one more time. "Hey, this is Edward."

There was silence on the other line. "Yes?" Her voice quavered.

"I wondered if you would like to stop by the farm?" My aunt nudged my sore ribs and whispered something in my ear. "And come for supper?" I parroted.

"If you're ok with that, I guess. What time?" she asked.

"Four?"

"Ok, see you then." Then Tabitha hung up the phone.

I decided to wait for Tabitha on the wrap-around porch, once again covered in a ridiculous poncho and drinking a cup of tea. My burns stretched with every rock backward, and a searing pain crossed my skin. The doctors said pain was good for burns, so I embraced it.

I pictured something in my mind's eye within my absent-minded stare—a vivid illustration. I was hunched over, and the Automaton had his hand on my back. Then once the Automaton saw that I was fine, he patted my shoulders and moved to sit beside another person: Jason. Then Jason ripped the Automaton apart, causing a collection of metallic parts to fall to the floor. In response to this, the Automaton magically reassembled himself and then calmly sat beside Bill. How was Bill?

A blue sedan pulled up the steep incline to the steps of the porch. My sister got out wearing sunglasses even though the sun was beginning to set behind the mountain. I patted the chair next to me and said nothing. She sat there rocking back and forth, tapping her index finger on her armrest.

"I've come to a realization," I started. "I'm not happy with how life is going, and it needs to get better; I must get better. I'm sick of being tired, and I don't want problems." I looked over at her to see if she had any expression, but there was none, so I continued. "I'm mad at you because you and Mom lost it after Dad died, and I was stuck looking after Mom. Did you know that she was going to jump off the railing? I caught her one day." Once again, I looked at my sister, and there was no emotion. "I dropped out of school to look after her and ended up here. Fortunately, I've met some very nice people who have helped me grow up, expand my mind, and take responsibility. I'm too tired to be mad at you, so can we figure this out?"

She started to twist a silver ring around on her index finger. "Yeah."

"So that's it? After all that, and you don't have anything to say?"

Tabitha started bawling uncontrollably. She got out of her chair and moved beside me, hugging me and crying into my poncho. I was completely uncomfortable with this, but I managed to hug her back. Who is she to come back to me and dump all these feelings? I caught this thought and examined it. Isn't this what I asked for?

"Edward, I'm pregnant, and my boyfriend left me. I've been living alone for the past couple of weeks. I'm at the motel now, but I've been living in my car before Cherry Lake." She looked up and forced a fake smile through teary eyes, which quickly turned back to crying.

It was as if the lightning had hit me once again. How many times must lightning strike? Why was I her lightning rod? Perhaps the Sunday before was a trial run for today. I was stunned and dumbfounded. I didn't know what I could do, so I cried, something I hadn't learn how to do until I worked with Dr. Winters.

What can I do? I'm just a kid—no, I'm a man. There's something I can do about this. But what now? What can I do at this moment? I thought back to what Dr. Winters taught me.

It's ok to cry.

It's ok to feel.

It's ok to encourage.

So that's what I did. "I love you, sis, and I'm proud of you." I felt those words were genuine enough, even though I felt uncomfortable saying them. After we composed ourselves, I asked her, "Do you wanna go in? There's good food."

Wiping her eyes, she responded, "Yeah."

I decided to take the five-gallon pail as a chair and let Tabitha have a guest seat. I opened the door for her, and we walked in and sat down. Tabitha didn't say much. She didn't talk about her pregnancy, job loss, or boyfriend. Whenever my aunt or uncle would ask her about something in her future, she would respond, "I don't know yet."

We didn't talk much about what had happened between Dad, Mom, Tabitha, and me; most of the conversation was about Aunt Emma's new farm projects, Uncle Matt's work on the ski hill, and my time at school. I was honest that I was barely making it, but Tabitha didn't tease me or mock me. Between bites of corn, she said, "Good for you." I also told Tabitha about my new friend Adam and my experience with the emu and Jason. I finally closed my story with Leah's funeral.

Tabitha finished her meal first. She began to speak, and as she did so, she uncomfortably shifted her utensils onto her plate and leaned on the table.

"First, I would like to say thank you for looking after Edward. My mother and I have not been well over the past couple of years, and I wish I knew then what I know now. So once more, thank you."

My aunt responded quickly, "Our pleasure."

"He's a good guy," my uncle affirmed and gave an affectionate punch to my shoulder. This caused me to wince in pain.

"I'm wondering if I could talk to you two alone after

supper? I would like to tell you why I'm here."

"Absolutely," my aunt responded. "Edward, would you mind taking the compost to the pile?" She pointed to another pale on the front porch. "How long do you need?"

Tabitha responded, "Only about ten minutes."

"Ok, Edward, would you give us some time?"

"Sure," I responded. I didn't know precisely what Tabitha wanted to say, but I wondered if she would tell them about the baby, her boyfriend, or being homeless. After finishing my supper, I wobbled out of the doorway, picked up the compost bucket, and made my way past the barn and to the compost pile. It didn't stink as bad as one would imagine. The summer heat caused everything to dry out nearly instantly. These days it was quite cooler as winter loomed near, and the nights caused everything to freeze.

I tossed the contents of the bucket into the pile.

"Have a nice trip?" a deep, raspy voice questioned. I nearly jumped out of my skin. I instinctively swung the bucket in the direction of the voice.

I turned around to identify who it was. Of course. It was the Automaton. Mr. Chorales. This time he was covered from head to toe in blue paint. It drenched him from top to bottom. It looked rather horrific in the diminishing light of the day.

"What happened to you?" I asked and gestured to the wet paint dripping from his metal mechanisms. "Aren't you going to seize up?"

He didn't move at all in response to that question. Mr.

Chorales just opened the diaphragms of his copper irises and asked, "What happened to you?"

Still annoyed at his avoidance of my question, I responded, "You know what happened. You always know what happened." I ran my fingers through my hair and turned away with a sigh.

"Did you figure out who I am?" the Automaton asked with excitement rattling down his neck.

"Yeah, I think I did, at the hospital. You are me—me in the future."

The Automaton snorted and shook his head back and forth, rattling gears in his head. A bolt came loose from inside and fell into the nearby compost heap.

"Almost, quite almost," he managed to say with some disappointment.

"No?" I was shocked. I thought I had managed to fit everything together.

"Nope, I'm not you—although part of you is part of me, it's complicated."

"What should I do about my sister?" I asked.

"What does she need?" he responded.

"I don't know . . ."

"What do you need?" the Automaton asked.

"I don't know . . ." I repeated myself.

"Then perhaps instead of finding the answer, you should figure out what riddle you are trying to solve. What type of game are you playing?"

"This isn't a game." I pointed my finger at his chest and

hissed through my teeth.

"Of course it is," Mr. Chorales insisted as he wiped a painted wrist on the back of my hand. "It is the game of dominance. The one you have been practicing throughout your whole life. Not dominance of others nor self-tyranny, but rather a game of games that justifies your existence."

As the Automaton finished his last words, I saw him take a couple of steps backward, and his head, arms, and torso fell apart onto the ground. Then rust began rapidly spreading from his left arm to his right. He calmly closed his eyes as if going to sleep and let the rust dismantle him completely. The reddish metal sunk into the soil, leaving the blue paint behind. A couple of seconds later, the blueish tint was also gone; this was absorbed into the ground. I was standing there with an empty compost bucket and was not shocked. The oddities of the Automaton had stopped catching me off guard because I was expecting the unexpected. As I approached the house, I noticed that my sister had moved her car beside it. The giant pig snuggled the vehicle's rear end in a deep sleep. I wiped the blue paint off my hand on a small pile of leaves.

Leaving the bucket on the front porch, I walked in. My uncle was waiting there, eating a doughnut. "Ed, we've got a dilemma. Tabitha told us everything that she told you, and now we gonna let her stay with us. I know you were here first, but I wondered if it wouldn't be reasonable if we set up a bed down here for you. Then Tabitha could have the upstairs bedroom. We aren't too certain how long she—or you, for that matter—will be staying with us."

"Yeah, that's ok."

My uncle raised his eyebrows. "Are you sure?"

"Yeah," I answered, although that wasn't entirely true. I was secretly excited about my own bedroom tonight after staying a couple days at the hospital. We brought down my suitcases and set up a small bed that expanded out of a chest. The TV with a hole in the screen was moved out to the porch and covered with a blanket. I didn't think the blanket would help with the rain, but I don't believe my Uncle Matt intended to fix it. That night, I remembered the first time I came to the farm. I was angry and burnt out. Now I was just burnt. That was a whole lot better.

I closed my eyes; it was peaceful. Not because life was perfect but because I felt that I had finally found a way to navigate the rapids of this uncontrollable river. If I could describe the peace, it was like a bloom within my body, moving from my heart to my arms and legs. This peace washed over me and delivered me to the morning.

*

Now that it was nearing the middle of October, I felt I was in the rhythm of school, work, and chores. Bill wasn't at school, and I didn't ask about him. Naturally, the whole town knew about me getting hit by lightning. The emu kid was finally taught a lesson by God. This experience turned me into a type of celebrity with my classmates. Kids that would have never talked to me started to smile and wave. In the grade twelve class, I was welcomed back. I had a feeling that this event was one to be remembered. I hoped that Bill's wasn't.

Honestly, I loved all the attention that I was getting. I'd kept a low profile at the beginning of the year. As I increased my confidence, I wondered about talking to other people. Navigating social complexities became a game to toy with, not just something to be avoided.

On Tuesday, October 22, my first class of the day was resourcefulness. Ms. Bronson walked us down to the lake and taught us to fish. Specifically, she taught Jason and me, since the rest of the class was evidently excellent at casting off from the shore. Before I even had my bait figured out, some grade nine kid had already caught a trout. Seeing it reminded me of the eagle that slapped its fish against the vehicles. As soon as the kid waved the trout above his head, Ms. Bronson forgot that she was helping Jason and me set up our fishing gear. Her excitement was palpable. She seemed like she was a little kid with her first fish.

"So, did you really get zapped?" Jason hissed without looking at me. I looked at him and didn't know what to make of his question. This was the first time he had said anything to me since he'd choked me for ratting him out. He still avoided my glare while fighting with a new lure.

"Here—look," I demanded his attention and gently lifted my pant leg. This revealed a dark red burn.

Jason chuckled. "Yup, I guess you did. Say, what were you doing in a lightning storm to begin with? You don't seem to be the type of idiot that would be out there for no reason."

I was a bit shocked. No one else had asked me that. Maybe they wondered, but no one said anything.

"Bad luck," I responded.

"Hm." He grunted in an unconvinced manner.

I looked down at the crayfish lure in my hands. "How's your dad?"

"Good, as always; that never changes."

"How are you?"

He looked at me and rolled his eyes. "The same."

Nothing else was exchanged between us. The tension was still there. I think that Jason was angrier at getting caught than needing to volunteer. When I told the police officer, I was lumped into the same camp of betrayers that Jason had made in his mind. I would sit there alongside his father, mother, and everyone else he knew. Was there anyone that he trusted besides himself? Probably not. Why would he?

# Chapter 18

November came in like a breeze. The days became shorter, and a gentle wind with a bite swirled through the mountains and valleys. Their tops became dusted with snow while the farm and Cherry Lake still bathed in autumn leaves. While some trees dropped their leaves, other evergreens popped out of the forest, standing proud while clothed in a royal green. The wildlife was still very active. Black bears were fat and ready for hibernation, while doe and their fawn could move about quicker than months prior. Tabitha helped out at the farm as much as she could. She was also working at a diner serving breakfasts and lunches while I was at school. Her little bump showed more, and her skin seemed to have a golden glow. She still seemed nervous and stressed, but I think she found some security at the farm. I noticed that she appeared to be extra kind to me. I reciprocated that, and it seemed to help us move through our past. Things didn't feel perfect, but everything was good enough.

My burns healed at a near-miraculous rate. The doctor thought it was because of my age and health. I still had some trouble gaining back feeling on the insides of my feet, from the arches to the tips of my toes. I also recovered my marks in school from the week I had missed in the hospital. I think this was because my teachers marked me easier, sent additional instruction home, and often stopped by my desk when we were working. Since the lightning strike, my confidence had shot upward. People began to notice me, and teachers took the time to help me more often. More importantly, I seemed to really get success for my effort. I would have gladly done it again if this was the benefit of getting hit by lightning. Since August, I've noticed my muscles have been getting stronger from farm work. I could work harder and longer. It probably helped that I stopped smoking after being hospitalized. Being there, bedridden, didn't give me much choice. Also, sleeping in the living room didn't give me opportunities to slink away to satisfy my addictions. My skin started to clear up too: I was beginning to look healthy.

My mind was still swimming with questions: Why did Leah have to die? Why am I part of the Automaton, and he is not me? Where's Mom?

On November 7 of 1995, I got the answer to the last question. A public mailbox was at the bottom of the road leading up to the farm. Adam's father was driving us home from school, and we got out of the truck to check the mail. I opened my aunt and uncle's box, number 32. There were some newspapers, coupons, a postcard, and a couple of letters. As we got back into the truck, I shuffled the letters and stumbled upon one with my name.

"Mel and Sons Property Management. Who's that?" I asked as I inspected the letter.

"Hmm?" Adam's dad questioned as he drove up the dirt road.

"Unit 57 of Eavestons Estate is to be vacated before December 15? That's where Mom and I used to live. What do they mean?"

"I guess that's their way of saying that you and your mom need to move out. Maybe more of your mother since you . . . you know . . ." Adam slowed as he approached this topic.

"Yeah, yeah . . . I gotta deal with the stuff. But where's Mom? Isn't she there?"

"If I were you, I'd ask your aunt. She seems to know more than the average person."

My mother was moved to a hospital, which was the last time Aunt Emma knew of her location. When we called the hospital, we discovered that she had been discharged to a long-term psychiatric care facility. From there, the managing company used my Aunt Emma as an emergency contact to send the letter to us.

"Well . . . what now?" I asked as I pushed my chair away from the kitchen table.

Aunt Emma shrugged. "I guess a road trip? I'll call the

school and tell them what's happening; we will make this a quick visit. I can't just leave the farm; your uncle is about to finish the ski hill. He can't let a single day pass."

"What about Tabitha? She can drive."

"She can, but do you think she should?" Aunt Emma questioned.

I gave it some thought. "Nope. Definitely not."

"Ok, it's you and me, I guess. I want you to pack up four days' worth of clothes in a suitcase and get ready to go. I'd like to get a head start on the road tonight."

"Tonight?" I asked in disbelief.

"Yeah, we will have some help from neighbours to look after things here, and you've seen the amount of work required to run a farm."

"Yes, at least now I do." I couldn't believe how much a single page of paper had changed my week. At first, it was uneventful but now . . . travelling? Seeing my mom? Cleaning out the apartment? I packed clothes and food and filled the van with gas; Aunt Emma called her neighbours to let them know what was happening. Afterward, she phoned Uncle Matt and Tabitha, who were still at work. Aunt Emma slid underneath her unused white van and checked the coolant and oil levels, hoses, and other mechanical things that I didn't know much about. Finally, we packed the van and started down the steep road to the highway. This whole process took just over an hour.

As Emma drove, I wrote down our cleaning tasks, and we

nearly had our plans laid out before we reached Cherry Lake. We passed Salmon Arm, Revelstoke, Golden, and Banff. I noticed that Aunt Emma began to look tired once we arrived in Alberta. I tried to talk to her to keep her awake. I told her stories about my dad, growing up in the city, and what I learned in school. She seemed to perk up when she learned about my last few classes on resourcefulness. I told her about fishing, cleaning a gun, and tracking skills. By this time, it was dark, yet there was a faint glow in the distance.

The Rocky Mountains peeled back onto the foothills and flattened out even more. The soft glow appeared to grow in height, length, and width. Before we knew it, we passed the old winter Olympic ski hill. I marvelled at the giant ski jump. My aunt pulled into a nearby hotel parking lot. The lot's lights flickered an orange hue while snow and ice diffused the light amongst the ground. Television sets made the occasional room dance in a chaotic glow and colour dashes. This reminded me of my time back in Edmonton.

Aunt Emma unbuckled her seatbelt with a sigh. "I'm sorry, Edward, I gotta stop. If I go anymore, my eyes will go to sleep whether I want them to or not."

"No problem. We couldn't get there all in one drive. Especially since we didn't start until the afternoon." I gave a yawn and rubbed my eyes.

"We'll make good time tomorrow," she muttered as she unloaded her suitcase.

And she kept that promise. She knocked on my door at

6 a.m., and we were on the road by 6:30. She had already made breakfast for me after having some herself. This timing wasn't unusual because Aunt Emma was often up early to feed the animals and start the day. This wasn't the type of trip to break a schedule.

We continued our drive, stopping once at Red Deer for gas. When we arrived at the apartment building, it was 10 p.m. and the wind was howling. I didn't remember it being so cold here in Edmonton. I looked up at my old apartment: it was thirteen stories tall and created a looming impression. The entire building appeared grey without the slightest inkling of colour or nature. A single bare tree stood out front and seemed to quiver in the cold. The apartment complex looked more miserable than the first time I saw it.

Arriving at the office, we saw an ancient-looking man, who handed us a key and a dolly, which we took to the elevator. He seemed unimpressed by our arrival; perhaps it was routine for the suites to have transient movers.

*Ding-ding.*

The elevator doors revealed a heavy scent of dust and old people. I was almost surprised that I remembered where to go. It seemed a lifetime ago that I had stayed here, but it was only about three months in reality. A neighbour heard us walking down the hollow-sounding hallway and poked his nose out. He was dressed in all black; a bronze security chain was tense between the door and its frame.

"Not back for more, are you?" He gave me a chilly frown,

tilting his chin toward his chest and peered over his glasses at us. Those eyes had tinges of yellow and appeared sickly. As we walked past him, his pointed nose followed our direction until he could no longer see us.

I ignored him and opened unit 57's door. It creaked and groaned as I pushed the door inward.

A putrid smell came stumbling out the door like a ghoul, causing us to gag simultaneously. I pulled my shirt over my nose and walked in. It was filthy. My mom hadn't had too much time to mess it up, but I guess she did. There were rotting bananas on the counter, although hardly identifiable since the shape, colour, and texture had amalgamated with the yellowish-green '60s-style countertop. Upon inspecting the rooms, the kitchen area, bathroom, and my mother's bedroom, we discovered they were all a complete disaster. When I pushed my old bedroom door open, I was completely surprised by what I saw. The room was impeccably clean—the floor was vacuumed, and lines still striped the floor. The walls were washed, and the windows were spotless.

"Huh . . . look at this." I gestured my aunt into my old room. "I used to stay here."

She appeared shocked. "That's weird. Why do you think it's so clean here but gross out there?"

"I don't know," I said with frustration as I shut the door quickly to ensure that the filth from the rest of the apartment didn't seep into this area.

My aunt started in the worse place: the bathroom. It was

a tiny room, but there were piles of empty shampoo bottles everywhere, towels on the ground, and an overflowing garbage bin. The toilet wasn't flushed.

I started with the kitchen, cleaning out the fridge, taking a large garbage can and tossing everything out. Rubber gloves scarcely helped my disgust. The refrigerator and freezer contents were dumped into the trash without a second thought. While this was normal for most, I mourned the loss of food because I knew how precious it was. I made sure to snag a plastic bag out of the flour tub. There was precisely fifty-seven dollars.

At first, we didn't want to get rid of Mom's possessions, but we found that we didn't have much room in the van after getting her dresser in. Many things could have been good, but the neglect had rotted them to the core, making them unusable. We called a removal company, and a couple boys just older than myself helped carry the bed out to a dump truck. Finally, at the end of the day, we got everything stuffed into the back of the van. Nothing was left in the apartment except for a lingering smell. To take care of that, we cracked open a window.

We were exhausted from that day, plus our sense of smell was gone entirely. We looked up the facility where my mother was staying and picked a hotel near it.

"What do you think will happen when we see her? Do you think she will be better?" I asked as we watched a home renovation show on a restaurant TV.

"I don't know what to expect. She's been through a lot, and

you have too. I hope that being in the hospital helped her."

"Oh, it helped me." I said this with a sarcastic tone, but I wasn't joking.

"Maybe she got some meds to help her through this. Whatever happens, know that you are welcome to stay with us for as long as needed. I understand you're turning eighteen and graduating high school. Pretty soon, you will face lots of choices, and who knows if you'll even want to stay in Cherry Lake? Maybe you want to be back here."

I gave a chuckle. "I don't think I have a reason to leave. At least not yet."

"What do you want to do when you grow up?" Aunt Emma asked.

"I haven't given it any thought. Things have been bizarre for a while, and I have only started to think about the future. I don't know . . . I don't even know what I'm good at."

"True, but you don't need to figure that out right now. Here's my advice. Figure out how to make money first, and then decide what you'd like to do. It's easier to be creative when you're not starving."

"I guess I have a couple options. I could work for Uncle Matt a bit, or maybe I could join Sid and do some roofing. I'll figure it out."

As I unpacked in my hotel room, my thoughts swirled around where I would live and what I would do. For the first time, I wasn't panicking but fantasizing. Maybe I will buy a house. Or even get married and have kids. Would I be a good dad? Then my thoughts turned to my mom.

When I pictured where my mom was staying, I thought of asylums in old horror movies. I felt prepared to walk into a nuthouse full of dangerous people.

You can imagine my surprise when we pulled up to a building that looked more like a resort than a hospital. People were walking in a park, a snow-covered square situated in front of the building. In the middle of the area stood a circular fountain without water. I imagined that this would be a beautiful space in the summer. We walked up to the front of the hospital and pressed the buzzer.

"Please state who you are here for," a voice screeched loudly from the tiny speaker.

Aunt Emma leaned in. "Uh . . . there are two visitors here for Lisa Lancer."

"Excellent, please come in." Then the door clicked.

We opened the door and walked inside. The room seemed cozy; it was decorated plain but elegant. It reminded me of a royal ballroom. We approached a secretary who got up and shook our hands.

"Visitors for Lisa?" she asked.

"Yes, that's us," responded my aunt.

She took us down a long hallway to a door on the right. She knocked on it.

"Come in," sang the voice. As we walked in, I saw my mother sitting cross-legged on a single bed, drawing something on her lap. Her jaw dropped when she looked at my aunt and me, and she didn't say or do anything.

"Edward?" she asked in a quavering voice.

"Yeah, it's me, Mom."

"Why . . . why are you here? Why are both of you here?"

I responded with anger. "We needed to clean up the apartment." My mother's eyes drifted down in shame. She began to colour a little and then looked back at me.

"I've been sick."

I corrected her, "We've been sick."

At this point, she began to fidget with a blanket on her bed, twirling it with her fingers. "I'm so sorry for letting things get this way. I thought I had a hold of things, but it just got worse and worse."

"It's ok, Mom." I sighed, clearly emotionally blunted by her repeated offence.

She insisted, "I didn't do the right thing; I didn't look after you. I should have made you go to school, and I should have picked myself back up."

Doubts crept into my mind, and silence filled the room. I wondered about the apartment. "Why was my room clean?" I asked.

"I thought if I cleaned it, they would let you come back, and maybe you'd want to come back," she said with a genuine look.

This pierced my defensiveness and allowed me to feel what I needed. Tears started to well in the corners of my eyes, and I turned around.

This was when my aunt stepped in. "Edward's been doing

great at the farm. And it looks like he will be graduating in June."

"Good, good," she said in an absent-minded mutter. "Thanks for taking him in; I didn't have many choices. I'm glad that everything will work out. I'll repay you someday."

My aunt stepped forward, sat on the edge of the bed, and grasped my mother by the shoulders. "I'm just going to say this once: I appreciate the gesture, but it's not needed. This is what family does for one another."

My mother looked down at her drawing and didn't say anything. "When you cleaned up the apartment, did you find some jewelry?"

"Yes, and we have it in the van," Aunt Emma reassured.

"Ok, can you please take care of it? I can't have it in here; jewelry isn't allowed."

I thought it was a ridiculous rule, although it was a ridiculous circumstance. I wondered what other laws were in place here that I didn't know about. Whatever happened here, it seemed to be making my mom's life a bit better. At least she wasn't starving. I guess that's all one can ask for.

A nurse knocked on the door and smiled. "Excuse me, but only five minutes left of visiting time."

"But we just got here," I protested. "We have only been here for ten minutes."

"That's right," the nurse insisted. "We only have fifteen-minute visitations per day. If you want to come back, you can see her tomorrow."

I began to argue with the nurse. "We are going back home

today; we won't have the time to come by."

"Then I'm sorry, I can't help you." And then the nurse left.

My mother's eyes locked onto mine. "Edward, your sister is planning to move to Cherry Lake; please take care of her. I'm so sorry. Here, take this."

She got up, went over to her dresser, opened the top drawer, and pulled out a drawing. It was a drawing of an astronaut, and in the reflection of its visor was the earth.

"Thanks, Mom. Why didn't you draw at home?"

She smiled, looked up at me, and touched my cheek. "Because I didn't realize that I needed to."

That morning, at 10:27 a.m., we started back to Cherry Lake. It was a long drive, and we packed the van. We hit a red light several times, and some of the van's contents moved around and crashed. At one point, some glass shattered in the back.

# Chapter 19

It was nighttime when we arrived back at Cherry Lake. We had gone on an adventure, yet nothing changed. Aunt Emma and I decided to let the contents of the van sit overnight once more. I remember dragging my feet painfully up the stairs after hours of sitting. After all, we had only left two days ago.

I felt that my visit with my mom and cleaning out the apartment was hugely anticlimactic. Tabitha had a lot of questions. In fact, she had more questions than I had answers. I noticed a shift within myself from anger to sadness; how can you judge progress when measured in pain? I felt lost and in some type of in-between identity. I wasn't quite the son my mother knew, but I wasn't the man I needed to be.

Despite my tiredness, Tabitha and I sat on lawn chairs in the dark rafters of the barn with little dancing flames in our lanterns. There was a large opening where we could see the whole farm and the opposing mountain range. Silent snowflakes clumped together as they fell in the winter breeze. We were both bundled heavily in blankets, tuques, and jackets. A tin of dark chocolates and marshmallows sat between us. Despite the weather, it was the perfect temperature, and the farm sounds were muffled by the snow. It was as if the world was in its own snow globe. The animals who slept below us preserved the barn's heat.

"So, what's going to happen now? Mom's all proper, and I'm waiting for this thing." Tabitha pointed her finger at her belly bump. After staring off into blank space for a while, she started again. "Well . . . are you doing ok? This is weird."

I cracked a smile. "This is weird, but it's great." I gestured out of the window to the mountains.

She continued to pry. "What happened to you? Something changed."

I looked Tabitha in her eyes. "Do you want to know the honest answer?"

To this, she just nodded.

"When I came out here, I was surrounded by people who wanted the best for me. You know, they are really good people. Anyways, I was pretty bitter and angry about the situation, and I met someone here one night."

"Oooooh, was it a girl?" Tabitha nudged me with her shoulder.

I rolled my eyes and ignored her. "It was the Automaton."

"The what?"

"A man—who is made out of gears and metal bits. But it's a real man."

"You met a machine-man?" Tabitha mocked. "But he can't be real if he's a machine, a robot."

I brushed off her disbelief. "But that's the thing, he is real and isn't. I had difficulty getting past that detail too. The Automaton is real because I'm learning to be like him."

Tabitha's face turned from a joking expression to a severe and perhaps concerned look. "What did you learn from him?"

"Lots, he taught me to hold the hand of a dying person, how to ask questions, and how to sit beside someone who is mourning. I realized that life isn't just about me and that I need some purpose or meaning to my life."

My sister scrunched up her eyebrows. "I'm reading quite a bit since there isn't much to do once the chores and work are done. The TV isn't even working. I've been reading this book about a guy in a concentration camp. He said that people's purpose is what keeps them going."

"I'd like to read that book sometime."

"You'd like it." Tabitha launched chocolate into her mouth.

We just sat in silence, watching the nightscape evolve and unfold. We stayed in the barn rafters for a while and then returned to the house.

\*

At school the next day, Adam caught up with me as we were changing classes.

"Hey, there's a lady from the university coming to our farm today, wanna come over? She is doing a research paper on some planets and wants to use our telescope. Can you believe it? She said that she would show me the planets in the night sky." Adam's enthusiasm was insurmountable, so I gave in.

"Yeah, I guess. It will be cold, right?"

"It should be, so make sure you wear something warm." Adam twitched a little. He always had more energy than he knew what to do with.

The entire family and friends stood there on Adam's massive porch, sipping hot apple cider and watching the astronomer collect her data. There were about twenty of us on the porch, all standing in silence. All the lights were off except the astronomer's red flashlight in her left hand while she wrote notes with her right. She would flip through pages, sigh, and then put her eye back to the telescope's eyepiece. She'd obviously worked with this telescope before, moving knobs, adjusting dials, and pivoting it in a manner that resembled an expert ballroom dancer. Academic professionals like this were rare in Cherry Lake; we were more well known for our adult illiteracy rates than our scholars.

When I watched her, I began fantasizing about something odd and extraordinary: a fantasy I never had before. What if I became an academic? What would that mean for my future?

It would undoubtedly lend meaning and direction to my life; however, was that an option? I fantasized about sitting in a grand old library, a dimly lit room full of dust, students, and books. What would I study? Maybe finding something to learn is like falling in love? At first, it's romanticized and then intentionally chosen out of an inability to choose something else? I wanted to be that old man with a long beard who lives in a hut on the edge of civilization. A hermit who knows the secret of the universe. People would journey to learn wisdom and understanding. An Automaton? Not quite.

The astronomer broke my fantasy. "Ok, everyone, please line up here if you want to see the rings of Saturn." She indicated with her arms where she would like us to stand. Adam grabbed my arm and pulled me into line.

He leaned forward and hissed in my ear. "Can you believe it? And to think that once she is gone, we can figure out how to use the telescope." There was a lot of excited murmuring and pushing in line. As we got closer to the telescope, there were little gasping bursts, and I could see the astronomer's smile widening. She seemed to have more fun presenting the experience than doing her research. Finally, Adam and I stepped up to the telescope. He looked through, then gasped and pulled me down to the eyepiece.

I looked through.

It looked like a ball of sand hung amongst the abyss of space, rotating and swirling. The rings looked like a pair of ears, and I could see lines inside the belt. I took it all in and then moved out of my way for the next person.

"Wow! Could you believe that?" Adam said enthusiastically and whacked my back with a mitted hand.

"That was really something." I allowed genuine enthusiasm to seep through. I didn't really know what to make of the experience. I felt small and insignificant, and rightfully so. What is the reason that I'm here? Why is there something instead of nothing at all? I knew I was a spark of light that dimly fades as these large giants stand with time. It was a humbling experience, and I wanted more. Could I really understand who I was without looking inside me? Perhaps I had it wrong all along: instead of just looking inward to know myself, I should look outward toward art, science, and reading.

Is this how I construct who I am? If I ought to *know myself* . . . how? What would be my burden if I were to become a self-made man? What may I lose painfully so I can moult my shell of inadequacy and irrelevancy to relieve the suffering of others?

The following celestial behemoth was Mars. The Roman god of war was caped in a red glow straight above us in the sky. The entire planet looked like an ocean that had lost its water. There were asteroid craters. While I looked through, the astronomer told us of the massive volcano Olympus Mons on Mars. She said it was taller than Mount Everest— unbelievable. She excitedly continued to talk about 51 Pegasi B, newly discovered just the month before.

That night, I laid awake in my bed. My eyes focused on the cracks in the paint on the ceiling. What was my life supposed to be? I felt like many young people didn't have much direction in their lives. Something about the vast expanse of space helped me locate myself. There seemed to be a great line to straddle: a knowledge that whatever happens, it is small and insignificant compared to the grand scheme of things. I didn't know what the grand scheme of things really was, but would I get to decide some of it? From the start of the first note until the end of the last beat—what exactly is happening? Who is playing the instrument of the universe, and what is the song? From these thoughts, I disappeared into another dream.

I fell into a deep sleep, feeling entirely apart from my body. I was also falling asleep in my dream. My eyelids were heavy, and my heart was slow. I wasn't supposed to sleep, but I was so tired. In my dream, I woke up with my head on my books. At the top of the page, I looked down to *Introduction to Elementary Organic Chemistry* by R.R. Smith. I looked around and found myself in the same library I had imagined earlier; however, it was a little more natural this time. Somehow I knew it was a dream, but I wasn't in control. I was like a canoe without paddles; I just saw everything pass by, but I could think about it at the same time.

Beside me, a man about twenty-one years old had his head on the desk with his book propped up so that he could read it with his head down. Faint murmurings—similar to the lineup to the telescope, although less excited, filled the halls. I was in a university library, at least in a university that my subconscious had created. I had never been here before. Every wall was lined with books, and at the top of the walls was a window. The intense sunlight pierced through the library like a white knight charging through an army of darkness. Some dust swirled in these light streams like sparks twirling around a crackling firepit. I sat upright and looked around. I knew that there was somewhere that I needed to be, but where? Who was I in this dream? There was a small photograph outside the library on my desk. I investigated the reflection of the picture and saw my face. At least seventy years of age, I was an old man with round spectacles, a white beard, and a wrinkled face. It looked like a happy face. I got up, gathered my books, and headed out of the library for no reason other than inner provocation. The sun was blinding, and I didn't look upward. I scurried from one building to another. I finally got to the building I wanted. Walking down, I saw Lecture Theatre 12.

Yes. That's right, I thought to myself.

I walked down the right side of the aisle and stopped at the front. From there, I put a button on the collar of my shirt. I pressed it; it identified my thumbprint, lit up blue, and said, "Welcome, Dr. R. Smith; your voice is now connected."

I shuffled my notes as the class quieted down. Then I proceeded to speak.

"Welcome back, everyone. As you may have already seen,

your midterm evaluation marks are posted on your course page, and well done to all of you. If you have questions about your grade or the test, feel free to ask me after the lecture. If you have a book in your hands, please turn to page 119— that's page 111 for our digital friends. Today's lecture will be tough, so if you have questions about it, please raise your hand before I move on to another topic."

I proceeded to give the lecture in my dream. I was somehow encapsulated by the ebb and flow of the process. I felt alive and excited to share something good I had learned with someone else. A couple of students fell asleep, but it was worth it because a couple students stayed on the edge of their seats throughout the lesson. A pair of twins were goofing around in the second row. After I was done, a student shook my hand and thanked me for teaching.

I woke up to the sound of a pig snorting.

Since I slept on the pullout bed, I could hear most of the animals as they got up in the morning. The pig was one of the loudest alarm clocks. It could wake me up using either ends.

What an odd dream . . . I was a professor, and I was able to teach something. I had never thought of myself as someone who would be good at teaching or even have something to offer. I wondered about this. One dimension of the dream that popped out at me was the prestige of the vocation. I was in a high-end school, the type of place that spits out great people who go on to do great works. There was something luxurious about the opportunity to be part of these people's lives. This allowed me to think back on my own life. Who exactly was a part of my journey? Who helped me? I thought back over the past couple of months, and many names came to mind.

Then Dad came into my thoughts. He did quite a bit with me before he died. Perhaps in a way, he was teaching me how I could be a person who survives his father's death. That is what happened, after all. At this time, I expected myself to feel moved—perhaps sad or excited. Maybe I was even bitter that the dream had ended, and I had to return to reality. I didn't feel any of those things.

I sat on the couch with the early sun rising, birds chirping, and a cup of black tea in my hands. The warmth from the cup was comforting. I just felt grey—no emotions, just a foggy head.

I pondered that dream for the rest of November and began fantasizing during the day. One day, I could be a wise professor standing on a stage with people congratulating me. I would enable future generations to pave their way forward. And of course, I would make lots of money. I picked up all the university and college brochures available at school: I wanted to learn something. Badly. Not for myself, but so that I could jump into my dream and continue from where it took off.

Adam approached me at the library. "My friend, whatcha lookin' at?"

"None of your business." I curled the pages so he couldn't

see what I was reading, but he wrestled the pamphlet away from me anyway. Keeping me at arm's length, he read out loud.

"Southern Alberta University? Whatcha getting at? You wanna be a bona fide academic?"

Adam handed back the brochure and gave me a jab between the ribs.

"Cows and pigs ain't good enough?" he teased with a smile.

"I've been thinking," I began with a serious tone.

"Oh no," Adam joked.

"Yeah, I wanna teach something."

"You could teach Sunday school," Adam still joked.

"Not that," I said promptly.

"Then what?"

"It sounds silly, but I want to teach as a professor," I said with pride.

"Before you go ahead and do that, you'll need to know something. Are your grades good enough to get in?" he responded with seriousness.

"Definitely not," I concluded honestly.

"Then why are you looking?"

"'Cause I want to teach."

"All righty there. Say, do you have everything you need for Monday?" Adam changed the subject; I think he didn't believe me. This temporarily derailed my ambition and made my mind spiral into worry and excitement.

Monday was our winter camping trip with our

resourcefulness class. We had two days to learn survival skills and camp overnight. I wasn't looking forward to it, but I was willing to give it a shot. A couple months ago, I wouldn't have even thought I would try winter camping, but here I was. About to enjoy the cold.

# Chapter 20

I assumed I had everything I needed for winter camping, or at the very least, that Aunt Emma and Uncle Matt would. However, I didn't have snowshoes, a hatchet, and winter boots.

"What about a tent? A tent wasn't on the list. Where will we sleep?" I muttered to myself and wondered. Aunt Emma and Uncle Matt could get me a sharpened, ancient-looking hatchet, but I didn't have boots or snowshoes. It wasn't that I had forgotten my boots from my apartment in Edmonton; I'd never owned any to begin with.

I remember waiting at the bus stop in winter. My toes would go numb, and the slush from the road would cling to my pants. When the slush would eventually melt and dry, the ankles of my pants would become crisp, grey, and crusty like hardened, crumpled newspaper. This lack of footwear never bothered me around the farm; I used black rubber boots to do my chores during the winter.

Once again, Adam's father took us to the New-to-You used to store to see if I could find a pair of secondhand boots. Those were on the top floor of the store. Despite my hopelessness, I found a single pair of boots, with the price tag still on, new ones with waterproofing and everything. Adam could hardly contain his excitement.

"Amazing! New?" he mused. "Honestly, that's not too bad—a little more than regular boots, but these look brand-new."

I tried them on beside a stuffed coyote who looked at me with its pearly glass eyes.

I wasn't as lucky when it came to the snowshoes; these were behind the cash register. They were old. As in, they were probably the first snowshoes made. The only new part of them was the two right-hand foot bindings. However, there was a left and right snowshoe. That's ok, I tied them on with the new boots. The one snowshoe went on rather well; however, the second one was a bit of a contortionist's game. In the end, everything worked out, and I was ready.

Our trip began by loading our gear while students were stuffed three to a seat into the front two-thirds of the bus. I sat squashed up between the window and a mammoth of a classmate named Marco. Again, I watched Cherry Lake disappear and the yellow school bus weave through the snowy mountains. Even the road was lightly dusted in snow; the landscape looked like white Martian mountains. Despite the palpable energy of the bus and deafening noise level, I rested my head and watched the trees pass in peaceful bliss. Sounds started to drown out, and I saw something I hadn't noticed in a long time. I notice the reflection of my eyes in the window. They were the eyes of a person older than me. The glint of excitement had gone somewhere. I noticed the person behind those eyes. It was a strange experience to realize the gratitude of an indescribable change.

The bus pulled into a parking lot beside a lake, and the students eagerly pushed themselves outside their cramped seats. Ms. Bronson was wearing a burgundy snowsuit and tossing everyone's gear out of the back of the bus. An ear-piercing screech continuously filled the air: this was the emergency alert letting the bus driver know the back door was open. Once we got our gear and snowshoes on, we crossed the lake. I was excited about snowshoeing but quickly discouraged after seeing how slow we moved. During the first hour, everyone was talking. Marco spoke to me, and we continued our conversation from the bus. He liked to talk about his family from Italy and their companies there. When the forty-five-minute mark hit, everyone became tired, and I looked down at my two snowshoes while walking. I caught a snowshoe and tripped. I looked up around me to see if anyone else noticed. All fifteen of us had hunched backs as we watched our feet shuffle through the snow. I looked back down and kept going.

When we eventually reached the other side of the lake, we stopped for lunch: peanut butter and jam sandwiches. We also had some hot apple cider from a massive thermos that Ms. Bronson pulled from her backpack. Then we started again, up the very steep incline of a mountain. At this time, we pulled off our snowshoes and hiked in our boots. I didn't have anywhere to store my snowshoes, which cut into my hands. Up we went; it took about the same time as the lake. I caught myself feeling surprised that the school allowed this trip. We crested the top of the mountain and shuffled down an equally steep slope to reach a lake. This lake was considerably smaller than the previous one, but judging from the nearby mountains' height, it would be deep. From there, we put our snowshoes back on. Once we were on the far side of the second lake, some of the class tried to make a fire while the other half made four quinzees.

I was on one of the quinzee-making teams. Ms. Bronson showed us how to do it. First, we stacked a pile of packed snow as tall as we were, then we dug down the snow to the ice on the lake. From there, we made a tunnel inward and then upward. Inside, there was a large slab of snow where we put our sleeping pads and sleeping bags. I had doubts that it would work; after all, I felt my hands frozen to the bone. When we finally finished the quinzee, it was dark, and our team made our way to the raging campfire situated on the edge of the lake. The meal for the night was canned noodles reheated by the fire.

Jason sat down heavily beside me at the campfire. By all accounts, it should have been miserable: I was cold, hungry, tired, and confident that I wouldn't have a good sleep. But something about the process made me satisfied.

"Edward," he grunted.

"Jason," I responded with minimal excitement.

"They should have told us about this miserable trip before we signed up for this class." Jason took his feet out of his boots and pulled off his socks. They were drenched in water; he must have gotten some snow in his shoes while making the quinzee. He placed his socks on his boots and rested them beside his feet near the fire. I saw his new boots cut into his ankles, causing them to blister.

"So, what are you going to do over Christmas?" I asked.

"You'll see," he spat with hate. The hairs on the back of my neck stood up. I figured he was just playing around with me, so I ignored it and ate my noodles.

"I'm getting out of here once and for all," Jason muttered.

"Yeah?" I asked through a slurp.

"Yeah."

A moment of silence passed, and I could see Jason was smiling. As the flames leaped into the air, the flashing lights lit up his manic face. It was unnerving.

He turned and sneered at me. "Still hanging out with that hillbilly Adam?"

"Yup, he's a nice guy. A little weird, but that's ok," I defended.

"Loser," Jason sighed.

I put down my fork and turned to Jason. "What is with you?"

He continued to provoke. "What do you mean? I'm just telling the truth."

"Nah, you're just cynical and resentful." I absolutely lost it. "You need to grow up. So your dad doesn't love you as much as he loves his little ski hill—so what? If I had to pick between an icy hill or you, I'd pick the hill any day."

Jason just scoffed and then smiled. "That's rich coming from your background. Yeah, you heard. The whole town knows about your sister. There's a rumour going around that she's knocked up. Is there a father in the picture? Probably not with your family's standards."

I wanted to punch him square in the face. He probably wanted to do the same to me. I got up and walked straight into the woods in the dark of night. It reminded me of when I ran away from my sister at the farm. I didn't go as far this time. I climbed until I could see the lake and fire below. I sat on a fallen log, fuming with anger. I could only picture Jason's stupid smiling face, and I couldn't get it out of my mind.

"Howdy, partner," said a voice beside me, and I felt my heart jump up through my lungs. The Automaton. Although it was dark, I could see the moonlight reflect off his shiny, polished surface.

"What do you want?" I snarled.

"Not much; what do you want?"

"To teach him a lesson." I gestured down the hill and sighed heavily. "I don't get it. Sure, I bet his dad is a jerk, but his dad's not dead. And sure, his mom left them, but at least he knows his mom's alive."

"You think he's resentful?"

"YES—he's an immature, resentful jerk," I replied.

"And? So what? There are lots of immature, resentful jerks in the world. You used to be one of them. You still are one of them when the day isn't going your way."

"I'm getting better." I felt an icicle of shame grow down to my heart.

The Automaton outstretched his arm and waved toward Jason, mimicking me. "He's getting better. What is the reason you reacted strongly?"

"I don't know. I think . . . I think . . ." Suddenly, the answer I had in front of me wasn't clear, and I became confused. I didn't have an answer.

The Automaton responded for me. "You were upset—not for him, but for yourself."

"Yeah, I guess."

Mr. Chorales rattled one of his ears. "You guess? It's absolutely about you—everything is about you, except when it's not. This is a lesson for growing up. Some get it; others don't. Some learn it when they are on their deathbed in the last few days of living."

"So, what am I supposed to get?" I asked.

"The lesson here is that you can choose your response. He

will poke you where you hurt. He will test you because he wonders if you will buckle. If you buckle, then he knows that you can't be trusted."

With that, the Automaton gave a cackling laugh and quickly leaned back and fell into the deep snow, causing it to burst upward. And then he was gone. My cold breath hung in the air before dissipating toward the full moon.

After collecting myself, I got up, returned to the fire, and sat beside Jason. He seemed shocked but didn't say anything. I think the choice to sit beside him spoke loudly enough. The light from the fire flickered up, causing Jason's face to look twisted and dark. His brown, piercing eyes just stared off into the fire, seemingly fantasizing.

The quinzee was warm, with three other boys sharing the dome-like structure. I snuggled into my sleeping bag, trying to get comfortable. I felt disturbed as I fell asleep, as if I could smell something was about to happen. I didn't know what Jason was up to, but I didn't want any part. As I closed my eyes, the disturbing feeling in the pit of my stomach began to shrink, only to be filled with cold and tiredness beyond comprehension.

*

"And I eventually fell asleep." I summarized my camping experience for Dr. Winters.

"Did Jason say anything else, or was that it?" she responded, shifting in her green cloth chair. We were playing

Go Fish on a coffee table in a deserted hallway of the hospital.

"That was it!"

"Wow! Do you think he will do something, maybe hurt himself or someone else?"

"Definitely not. He won't hurt himself because I think he's too self-absorbed. And that's probably why he wouldn't hurt anyone else—because he wouldn't like to get caught."

"So, shifting the conversation back to us. As this is the final session, is there any unfinished business you want to draw attention to?"

"No . . . not really. I have found these sessions helpful. I know I'm done for now, but I think there is more I will need to return for."

"Sounds fine with me. Go fish."

I picked up a card and asked, "How long will you be here?"

"Well, I don't exactly know. I think for the foreseeable future, I guess. I don't want to move away anytime soon because, like you, Edward, I just got used to living here."

"If I come back, I hope I can see you," I said with genuineness.

Dr. Winters cracked a smile. "Thank you, I appreciate it."

"Really, things have been getting better," I insisted.

"Honestly, I think you give me too much credit. You're the one that did all the work." I thought of these words, and I didn't know if they could possibly be true. Was I the one responsible for putting in the work? It didn't seem that simple, but it made sense that it was part of what happened.

As I walked out of the hospital and down to my uncle's metalworking shop, I felt disappointed and vulnerable now that I couldn't regularly see Dr. Winters. The training wheels were off, and I was on my own. This time, I felt ready.

*

On December 16 of 1995, nearly the whole town and nearby ones congregated at the bottom of the ski hill for the grand opening. We had snow for a while, but I guess there were a couple more last-minute details to wrap up. There were camera crews from several news outlets, and the ski lodge was in full swing, packed full of excited winter sports enthusiasts who got a significant discount on their stay. They made up a considerable portion of the crowd, wearing bright clothing that looked anything but fashionable. These people were louder than the townsfolk and wore smiles as their uniform.

As Jason said, his father didn't do this for the money. The entire area was finalized, and it looked fantastic. There was electricity in the air: what would this mean for the town? Indeed, more jobs, more tourism, and better opportunities. Cherry Lake had no reason for people to stop by it, and it seemed that the entire population came in through the hospital, lived their lives, and died in the hospital. The displacement was zero. Now that half of my school year was basically over, I wondered what this meant for me. Would there be a job for me to stay at Cherry Lake? Perhaps I could move out, and my sister and I could find a place together and leave my aunt and uncle's farm.

Suddenly, as we were standing in front of the stage, red fireworks went off in the background slopes of the hill. As this happened, the music got louder, and we all looked around toward a large stage. Jason's father jumped onto the stand, and the crowd cheered. Despite the chilly weather, he wore a grey suit and beamed summer energy. Several flashes from photographers went off, and he gave a pearly smile. He shined with charisma, pointed to several crowd members, and gave a thumbs up. He performed a backflip, which caused the crowd to rumble louder. He spread his arms toward the hill, lodge, and a giant sign that held the logos of the hill's sponsors.

He spoke into a microphone, and his voice echoed off the mountain behind him. "Welcome, everyone! Firstly, I would like to thank the town of Cherry Lake and my co-investors." He waved a hand to several people on the right hand of the stage. "Secondly, I would like to thank my son Jason for believing in me and my vision—why don't you come up here, Jason?"

Jason made his way through the crowd. I had a feeling in my gut from the other night. What was he saying on the trip again? He was dressed in a ridiculously puffy black winter jacket and had his hands in his pockets. Standing up there with his father, he looked absolutely miserable, and his eyes seemed to be fixated on someone in the crowd. I tried to see who he was looking at, but I couldn't trace where his eyes lay. Maybe the police officer? Then out of nowhere, he turned around and pulled something out of his pocket. It just looked like a bottle.

Then he lit it on fire.

Time seemed to slow down as the smiles within the crowd began to twist into confusion and terror. Jason's father contorted through the most significant transformation: displaying wide eyes and horror on his face.

Jason held the Molotov cocktail high above his head, and he threw it at the lodge. Fire and flames erupted everywhere across the wall of the ski resort. It was like a dragon blasting the wall area with its fiery breath. Several people screamed, and a police officer was already pushing through the crowd. Jason's booming laugh cackled and cracked. He raised his hands above his head in triumph. He didn't seem to care about getting arrested. He wanted to burn the resort to the ground, giving it his best shot. He desired a public spectacle: not planned as a midnight trip with a crowbar, gasoline, and matches.

But the fiery throw wasn't enough, because he'd missed a window or wooden wall. He simply hit a rock wall, and some flames danced on the snow below for a while before naturally going out. His cries of triumph changed to anguish as he noticed nothing was happening despite his flames. His father looked shocked, and the police officer dragged a very distraught Jason away. The crowd stood silent and looked at Jason's father. He regained his composition and displayed a convincing smile.

". . . And the show will go on! Please give a warm welcome to Mr. Bronson, our head of management. He will tell us what we can look forward to in the next couple of months, along with some summer opportunities."

Everyone just stood in shock while the blackened stone wall emitted wisps of smoke.

# Chapter 21

I thought of what had happened as I lay in my foldable bed that night. Undoubtedly, Jason was in jail—although, was he? He seemed to have become unhinged. I thought back to all my interactions with him. Didn't he say that he wanted to burn down the lodge? How long ago did he plan this? I rolled over in my bed; it was uncomfortable. The black cat laid at my feet. He got up, turned around, and sat down with a sigh.

Even though Christmas break started as quite eventful, it was slow after the start of the ski hill. I didn't have school, and the farm was very slow. We needed to feed the animals and clean; however, things were slower than in summer or fall. Since the ski hill was completed, my uncle gave everyone at the company a break as they had been working nonstop since August. He seemed to get a little rambunctious on the third day of vacation, beginning to fidget and fix things around the farm. He appeared less grumpy and more often in a silly mood. My sister's stomach had a discernible bump, indicating that she had been pregnant for a couple of months. This was more prominent since she was skinny. She seemed very busy at the restaurant and enjoyed it; after all, she had begun to establish a routine.

Most of my days started early with about one hour of chores. Then I would meet up with Adam, and he'd tell me all about wrestling and the stars he saw through the telescope. He seemed equally inspired by the astronomer's teachings, and his parents purchased some college textbooks. Most of the winter was spent reading books and playing board games. I had lost the sense of boredom from when I first moved here. Adam's father was even beginning to teach me how to ride horses. He seemed very laid-back and easygoing most of the time, but when it came to teaching riding, he was as strict as he could be. This was good because it forced me to be rigid and confident with my horse. Over Christmas break, I got the basics, and I was looking forward to the spring when we could go on a fair ride. At this time of the year, the snow was two feet high in some areas, which meant minimal horse-back riding, and most people stayed away from travel. The cold air was different here than back home; it was less harsh and had less bite. The snow was different too. Snowflakes were massive and floated down like tiny parachutes.

On Christmas Eve, the church hosted a nativity play. Uncle Matt, Aunt Emma, Tabitha, and I managed to stuff ourselves into the small truck cab and make our way down the mountain to the church. Usually, I wouldn't be interested in going, but since I was out of school and stuck at the farm, I was getting restless and wanted to see people. We arrived early to help set up, even though we weren't involved initially. Since we lived in a small town, it was customary to do that with any event. While I talked to Adam's father, a lady from the church approached me.

"Excuse me, dear, there was an accident on the side of the church, and I was wondering if I could get your help cleaning it up? Some props were moving around, and a window broke."

I looked at Adam's dad, wondering why she didn't ask him.

"Sure, I'll help out. Where are we going?" I asked.

"Just over here. We need to clean the inside and outside. Let's do the inside first because I don't want anyone hurt. You go down that hallway there and see it on the left. I'll be right there; I'll get a garbage can and gloves for you and the other boy."

As I walked, I anticipated who this other boy was. I hoped it wasn't Jason with the deepest sincerity. No, it couldn't be. He would definitely be in jail right now. He'd just turned eighteen, so he would be tried as an adult, and I didn't think his father would get him out of there anytime soon. I saw someone hunched over, picking up small pieces of a broken stained glass window. It was Bill. He wore black jeans and a collared golf shirt and began to pick up pieces of glass with one hand and put them in the palm of another.

"Hey," I said as I approached him. Bill turned his head and smiled—a genuine smile.

"Hey," he responded. I squatted down beside him and began to also pick the shards. It was awkward, but I remembered my regret during the funeral. I had to say something.

"Are you better, Bill?"

"Yes . . . I . . . got . . . better."

"You're not stuttering?!" I replied.

"No . . . I . . . got . . . help . . . for . . . that . . . and . . . more. Like . . . you . . . said . . . Dr. Winters . . . works . . . miracles."

"What happened?"

"My c-cousin . . . died . . . of . . . it, and I . . . couldn't think . . . of anything else. There . . . was . . . other stuff . . . going . . . on as well. I . . . was . . . sick."

The lady who brought me to the broken window showed up again and gave us some gloves and a large black metal bucket.

"Hey! Mrs? Can I keep this?" I pointed to the glass we dumped into the trashcan.

"I guess that's fine with me. Bring the bucket back, so you don't accidentally become a thief." Then she gave a laugh and walked away.

"I gotta ask—what made you better?"

"I thought . . . and had . . . a lot of time . . . I wondered . . . how Leah . . . made it through all . . . the g-garbage. I guess . . . she . . . had something I . . . didn't have . . . A purpose. After all

. . . anyone could . . . die for a . . . cause. But . . . not everyone . . . could live . . . for one." This instantly brought my mind back to several memories: the vision of my reaction, Jason's response, and Bill's reaction to the Automaton.

"Did you find your purpose?" I asked earnestly.

"I . . . will . . . then I can . . . find peace."

"Hmm. That sounds good. Notice the colours?" The bucket was perhaps the most beautiful in the world—a dance of colours appeared at the bottom, and the glass collection shimmered back sparkles of light. I knew I wanted to do something with it, but I wasn't sure what. I had no experience making stained glass windows; it was broken anyway. I just liked the colours, so I asked for them. After cleaning the church, I put my bucket in the corner of the boot room and hung my jacket above it. Bill and I arrived at the same time as the Three Wise Men. I didn't know much about the story, and the acting was terrible, but I felt I was at the right place at the right time. I also thought that I had real hope for the future.

That night I could hardly sleep. I had my glass bucket on the porch, covered with a plastic bag to keep all the snow out. The pig was sleeping outside the window and took deep breaths that reminded me of the washing of a tide. I felt excited for Christmas Day. We didn't attend church, but we always got together during Christmas. I knew that this was the first time that I would be away from my mother during Christmas and that Dad wouldn't be there, but I was excited to celebrate the birth of something new within us. Honestly, as childish as it seemed, I was excited to have gifts for the first time in a couple of years. Not only excited to receive them, but also to give them.

Christmas Day was even better than I expected. We went sledding with Adam's family, and his father set up a sled ride with horses for the community. Believe it or not, I was on one of those horses, guiding it to where it should go. We didn't go far, but I was ecstatic to have been able to go anywhere. The little kids shrieked and cried with excitement when I took the corners quickly. Their mothers would grimace in worrisome anticipation. One neighbour brought some authentic maple syrup, and we heated it on a small gas stove and then poured it on ice. Then we took popsicle sticks and rolled the syrup into a frozen lollipop. Hot apple cider and a stew soon accompanied it for lunch.

Just after eating, we headed to Cherry Lake to go skating. Walking off the boat launch onto the ice, I realized that the ice was remarkably smooth. Uncle Matt insisted on ice fishing and caught two lake trout. Aunt Emma drew a picture on her sketchpad and refused to show it to anyone. I just skated as fast and as far as possible. I turned around and peered back toward the docks. Little people were moving near the shore, and more families arrived, many of them with children.

Finally, the best part of the day came around. It was Christmas supper, just the four of us in Aunt Emma and Uncle Matt's tiny farm kitchen, but we had ham, stuffing, carrots, and much more food we'd grown throughout the year. There were candles around us, heating up the house, and the kitchen window by the stove was cracked to let in a breeze and cool the home down. As we finished our supper with black forest cake, my uncle leaned back, got up, and pulled something out of his coat pocket. It was two envelopes—one for me and one for Tabitha.

"One last gift."

I quickly noticed that my name on the envelope was in Mom's handwriting; it had always had a messy slant. I cautiously opened the envelope and saw my aunt and uncle giving smiles. Before I could open the letter, a small picture fell out. It was a photograph of my mom, dad, sister, and me. In that photo, I was about ten years old; I unfolded the lined paper and read quietly.

Dear Edward,

I can't find the words to describe how much I have let you and your sister down. I wasn't there when you needed me, and I'm unable to be there now. Tabitha told me about the baby, and I'm so excited for us. I realize I'm sick, and even though I'm getting better, it doesn't seem to be soon enough.

I'm so proud of who you have been able to become. Words cannot express how guilty and thankful I am that you cared for us. I'm ashamed to say that you became the parent instead of me. You were the responsible one, and I robbed you of the final years of childhood.

Please forgive me; I want our family to start new again. I don't exactly know what to write in this letter because I'm still working through grief and recovery, but I do know one thing. I love you, Edward. I love you with all my heart, and I need to be able to tell you that in person. So I promise I will keep working, thinking of you often.

Please remember me.

Love, Mom

By the time I reached the end, I authored the letter with tears as my stamp of approval and forgiveness, and my sister was also crying. What now? Where now? There were so many questions. I knew I was heading in a good direction, but I didn't know where. I leaned over and gave Tabitha a hug. I indeed couldn't ask for more in a day. I love you, Mom. I'm glad you're alive. Merry Christmas.

# *Epilogue*

It turned out that I could graduate early—around mid-April—not with excellent marks, but I was able to challenge the final exam halfway through the last portion of my grade twelve year. I got between 55 and 60 percent in all my subjects. Not bad for someone who missed the last half of high school. I also picked up an odd hobby: making mosaics. This was introduced to me at school during one English class. We had a project where we made a mosaic about one scene of Shakespeare's writings that we studied. In addition, we were supposed to remember and rehearse the scene. I spent countless hours working on the memorization in the workshop and the mosaic. We were supposed to use everyday items, nonconventional means of creating the scene. Thanks to Uncle Matt's metalworking shop, I gathered a bunch of scrap metal to recreate the stage with the dagger from Macbeth. This scene was a masterpiece in my mind, yet not the easiest to memorize.

Since the teacher was so impressed with my work, I decided to do a couple more experiments with wood pebbles from the creek, and then finally, my gaze rested on something from months earlier: A small white bucket of glass from the church's stained glass window. I had forgotten what was in the bucket, since it was mid-May. I poured the glass onto the table and arranged different shapes and angles. Finally, I had a eureka moment. I started drawing and noting what figures I had and planned a masterpiece. Using the church window, I created a picture of a rabbit—the rabbit—with a pocket watch. As I placed it together, I thought of my time at the farm. A memory came into place with each drop of glass:

The pig on the porch.

Archery with Adam.

Dr. Nialliv.

An emu with a necktie.

Roofing with Sid.

Sitting by Leah as she died.

The lightning strike.

Christmas.

I sat there reminiscing about the past ten months; they seemed like a lifetime ago. So much has changed—some things for the better and some for the worse. I'm leaning into my inner automaton: the part of me telling myself that it is ok. Life is complicated, tragic, and breathtakingly beautiful.

You could spite it for all you want, but you are stuck in the ballet with fate and fury, so you might as well laugh while you feel it. I learned that from Dr. Winters.

As I made it my mission to step into the Automaton, I began something I never thought I would do. I stood outside of a gated compound just past Kamloops. I carried a book in my hand, nodded, and smiled at a man in uniform who let me in. Since I had more time than I knew what to do with, I felt retired from being a student and somewhat lost. So I began to help those who were also lost. As I approached the familiar building, I was searched, but my aunt's van keys, wallet, and book were all I had. I waited in a small room until I was called in by a rather unfriendly-looking woman in her early twenties. I sat down and picked up a phone.

"Yes?"

"Chapter 9?"

"I think so."

I proceeded to read the next chapter about a lion and some children. We only had about thirty minutes, and then I was cut off by the same guard that let me into the room.

Tired eyes looked up.

"Same time next week?"

"Yes . . . Thanks, Edward."

"You're welcome, Jason."

Jason turned around and headed back to the door where he'd entered. And I returned to the farm. I'm sure he could get the same book from the prison library, but he never did.

Since I had some time on my hands, I also began to work more often at my uncle's metalworking shop, but that wasn't all. My most important job was down the highway in another town—specifically at their town hall from 7:30 to 9:00 at night.

I walked into a room filled with about six adults, two older retired men, one mother, a farmhand, and a pair of twins a little older than me.

One of the twins piped up. "What's on the menu today, professor?" he said, waving his hand toward one of my textbooks.

"Conjunctions," I replied with a smile before erasing the blackboard and flipping to page 22 of the book. Each adult shyly pulled out a pencil and some binders. Their writing was incredibly messy and had marks all around it. The spelling was wrong, and the only correct thing on the page was their name on the top right-hand side of the paper; I was incredibly proud. They placed a children's book on the table, the same book I was reading to Jason. We started by reading aloud, each person stumbling through each word but getting more confident as we rolled onward; illiteracy had no shame here.

With each word read and line printed, we floundered into new opportunities. An awkward dance, like the movements of the Automaton. It was the dance of a windmill: standing tall and strong while turning our faces toward the storm.